A Cheechako's View of

Alaska

To Pat
Enjoy this tour through
ALASKA!

God Bless you.

Ethel McMillian

A Cheechako's View of

Alaska

Ethel McMilin

TATE PUBLISHING & *Enterprises*

Tate Publishing
& Enterprises

Tate Publishing is committed to excellence in the publishing industry. Our staff of highly trained professionals, including editors, graphic designers, and marketing personnel, work together to produce the very finest books available. The company reflects the philosophy established by the founders, based on Psalms 68:11,

"THE LORD GAVE THE WORD AND GREAT WAS THE COMPANY OF THOSE WHO PUBLISHED IT."

If you would like further information, please contact us:
1.888.361.9473 | www.tatepublishing.com
TATE PUBLISHING *& Enterprises*, LLC | 127 E. Trade Center Terrace
Mustang, Oklahoma 73064 USA

A Cheechako's View of Alaska

This novel is a work of fiction. However, several, descriptions, entities and incidents included in the story are based on the lives of real people.

Published in the United States of America

ISBN: 978-1-5988689-3-7

07.01.25

Dedication

To my husband, Jack McMilin, for all
his help and encouragement.

Foreword

Using her many personal experiences and the adventures of her family and friends, Ethel McMilin, a resident of Alaska for 14 years, transports her readers to the exciting, beautiful world of Alaska. Only a "Cheechako" turned "Sourdough" could understand and tell the story of Elizabeth Sweeny, a city-girl from Los Angeles who finds herself married and relocated to the very different world of Alaska. Beth learns to admire and love her new home, but only after many trials and errors that many others have learned before. McMilin's use of true incidents and her down-to-earth storytelling lend credibility to the new bride's adventures and readers will find themselves chuckling at the antics pulled by some of Beth's new friends. *A Cheechako's View of Alaska* is a comfortable journey through a rugged, remarkable country filled with wildlife encounters and lively "sourdoughs" rarely experienced by those living in the lower "forty-eight".

Vonnie Volzer–Software Engineer–Boeing

Chapter 1

The Neighbor's Son

Elizabeth Vandermeer stretched her arms out in a long yawn and looked up from her lawn chair glancing at the noisy ruckus coming from her neighbor's house. Her eyes widened as she stared at the newcomer. Going into the Sweeny's front door was the biggest, cutest, burliest man she had ever seen. That had to be the Sweeny's son. Mrs. Sweeny must have told her ten times that her son was coming home from Alaska for a visit. How many times had she heard tales from Sarah Sweeny about the antics of her son? One thing about it, he was ever bit as good looking as his pictures that were plastered on the Sweeny's wall. The one and only child who monopolized any conversation she had with the Sweenys.

The thought had occurred to Beth that since he was an only child, what was he doing way up in the wilderness of Alaska with his parents down here by themselves? Somehow it didn't seem right. But the parents were proud of their Alaskan son and felt privileged that he came home once every year to visit them. It seemed as though this only child could do nothing wrong according to the doting parents.

Beth's family had moved from back east to the suburbs of Los Angeles, California. Her father's promised promotion was the determining factor that ended in a move across the states. No one was disappointed at the beautiful California scenery. It was different from Ohio, that was a given. They quickly adjusted to the big city life and felt right at home in Los Angeles.

All at once, Beth remembered that the Sweenys had planned to come get her when their son came home. They wanted the two to meet and they were not bashful about the proposal. They knew the two of them would get along famously and they wanted their son to enjoy his stay.

"You will come over and meet him, won't you, Dear?" Sarah had asked her just a couple of days ago.

"Why, of course. Just let me know when your son comes home and I'll come over." Beth had smiled at the two parents. Their plans were so transparent and they didn't even try to hide the potential matchmaking. Well, from what she had seen of the physical man, his good looks, his well proportioned physique, she could have been very interested. But Beth was not interested in an Alaskan. From the stories the Sweenys had told her, that place wasn't even civilized to live in. She was the first to admit that she wasn't the pioneer type. She was a city gal!

Joshua Sweeny walked out the front door and jaunted over close to where Beth was sitting in the lawn chair.

"I have been given orders to come over and make your acquaintance. I have been programmed to obey," he said with a grin. "My name is Josh and I'm very pleased to meet you, Miss Vandermeer."

Beth glanced up at the smiling giant and grinned. "Hello! The name is Beth. I'm pleased to meet you. Your parents have been very excited about your visit. They have mentioned you a few times in their conversation, in fact, quite a few times. You know that they think the sun rises and sets in you?"

"Doesn't it?" he grinned. "I happen to know a little bit about you as well. My mother's letters have been full of the neat little lady that lives next door. How I must meet her. How sweet she is. How beautiful she is. Do you know that this is one of the first times that I believe my parents have picked out a girl for me and everything they said about her is true? You are every bit as beautiful as my mother said."

Beth tried hard to ignore the blush that painted her face. Although she was not used to such blunt remarks, she managed to reply, "Your parents pick out your girls for you?" Beth looked up into the smiling face of the tall and evidently friendly neighbor.

"They try. This time they may have succeeded. I think I'm in love already. How about having dinner with me tonight?"

"You just got home. You need to have dinner with your parents and spend some time with them. You can't leave them on the first night home," Beth said in a scolding tone to her new acquaintance.

"My mother sent me over here to make a date with you. If you don't believe me, come over and ask her. She's rather fond of you and feels that if I don't hurry, you might just get away. Since I'm already in love with you, I think I agree with her. I wouldn't want you to get away!" Josh was looking at her with a wicked grin and eyes that seem to penetrate her thoughts.

Beth knew that Josh was teasing her, but wasn't quite sure what to say to the brash young man. "I ought to take you up on that ..."

"Come on, then." Joshua Sweeny grabbed her hand and pulled her up. "We'll go ask them."

"You don't want to embarrass your parents."

"Oh, it wouldn't embarrass them. They have often made dates for me before. I usually managed to dodge the ladies after one date. But this time, I don't want to dodge my new date. I've been smitten by the love bug," he said as he looked her square in the eyes.

"Do you say this to all your dates?" asked Beth.

"You're the first!"

"Why don't you invite your parents to go out to dinner with us, then? That way, you can spend some time with them as well as make the date they wanted you to."

"Come with me and we'll try to persuade them," Josh said taking her hand and pulling her toward his home. Once they were walking up the stairs, he dropped her hand. "I don't want my folks to think they succeeded too easily," he teased.

Beth wanted to crown him but felt that he was under as much pressure as she was from his parents to get acquainted. Josh opened the door and Beth stepped through saying her hellos to each parent.

"You finally have your son home with you now, Sarah. How long is he going to stay at home with you?" she asked trying to start a normal conversation rather than meet Josh's challenge to ask about the date.

"He will be with us for about three weeks and we want you two children to get acquainted while he's here. We thought it would be nice if you two went out to dinner this first night and got acquainted right away," Sarah explained and smiled at Beth.

"Only if you two go with us," Beth said. "It isn't fair for you not to spend the first evening with your son. You must come with us and pick the restaurant where you want to eat."

"That would be a nice idea, Beth, only we have an appointment that we can't get out of and we didn't want Josh to be bored the first night he's home. Won't you help us out, Dear, and go out to dinner with him? We should be through with our appointment by the time you two get back from dinner." Mrs. Sweeny came over and put her arm around Beth in a friendly persuading manner. Beth was stuck. There was nothing else to do, but accompany Josh to dinner. Not that the thought was so undesirable, but the young woman hated the feeling of being manipulated, something she had never enjoyed. However, Sarah Sweeny was a sweet neighbor and she would go along with the plans.

"Suppose I pick you up about six. That way we can do a little window shopping before dinner. My parent's appointment is at 6:15 and the people they have the appointment with will meet them here at that time. Would this arrangement be okay with you, Miss Vandermeer?" Josh asked with a smirk on his face. He had won and he knew it.

"Very well, Mr. Sweeny, six o'clock is just fine. Is this to be formal or informal?"

"Oh, let's make it informal, Miss Vandermeer. We Alaskans aren't into much fancy or formal dress styles."

As they bickered back and forth, Beth noticed both of Josh's parents had a grin on their faces. They were enjoying this all too much as far as Beth was concerned. She felt that she was the one that was getting the brunt of the joke. The Sweenys had been good friends and neighbors this past year and she enjoyed their company even though it was usually a one-sided conversation about Joshua. There was no way she would hurt their feelings even if she had to date ten of their sons. She was thankful that they only had one!

Chapter 2

The Prearranged Date

Josh was at the door exactly at six o'clock and Matthew Vandermeer welcomed him into their home. "Well, you must be Joshua, the Sweeny's Alaskan son. Come on in and make yourself at home. It's so nice to meet you after hearing so much about you. Beth should be down in a moment. Tell us a little about your state and what it is that keeps you up in the cold wilds when you could be enjoying the sunshine in this beautiful state. We have enjoyed our stay in California. The state offers every different type of climate there is and every different type of scenery. We have fallen in love with California. I suppose that is the way you feel about Alaska?"

"It most certainly is. You can't imagine the diversity of Alaska until you are up there and travel around. It rather grows on you and in time you realize it's the only place you want to live. You must plan a trip up there and bring Beth with you. I think she believes we all live in igloos and have no civilization at all." Josh had given Matthew a hearty handshake when Jean Vandermeer walked in the room.

"This is my wife, Jean. Josh was about to tell me some Alaskan adventures, Dear. Where is that daughter of ours? Is she ready to go?"

"Yes, Dad, I'm right here ready to go," Beth said as she walked down the stairs. "I thought it might be interesting to listen to some of Josh's tales about Alaska. Do you live in Anchorage or Fairbanks?"

"I'm afraid not. Both cities are too civilized for me. I have a cabin several miles out of Fairbanks in the boonies. It's nice quiet living. I keep working on my place trying to modernize it. In Alaska, that can be a slow process as the weather isn't always agreeable with building. But, the country grows on you. It's fascinating to see the ice fog, the northern lights, the crystallized ice that forms on the trees and bushes in the winter, the no sun in winter and the sun shinning most of the day in the summer. In the summer there are hills that are filled with different types of berries. So many blueberries and the best tasting berries you'll ever find. You must come up to Alaska some day and see for yourself." Josh realized that he had been caught up in his story telling and it was time that he took a breath and let the Vandermeers do some talking.

Matthew came over to Josh and put his hand on his shoulder. "You will come back, Joshua, and tell us more, won't you?" he asked.

"Be delighted to. I'll be home for about three weeks and should be able to visualize some of the wonders of Alaska so you can understand a little about my state." He turned to his date. "Shall we go now, Beth?" Josh asked and opened the door letting her step through. "We'll try not to be too late," he promised before closing the door.

"Take all the time you want," remarked Jean Vandermeer. By the grin on her mother's face, Beth could tell that she heartily accepted Josh as a suitable date for her daughter. More manipulation from her parents as well as Josh's!

When they walked to the car and slipped in, Beth remarked: "I'm a big girl now, Josh; I don't have to be in by ten."

"I know, but I wasn't just sure but what your parents were expecting me to bring you home early on the first date. Your parents don't know me," Josh remarked.

"There you are wrong, Mr. Sweeny. My parents have heard so much about you that they feel that they already know you. They have seen your pictures so many times and they know more about you than you would want them to. Your parents and mine are in cahoots about this, this … this … matchmaking. We're being manipulated by both your parents and mine. Didn't you see the pleased looks on our parents' faces?"

"My mom and dad seemed to be very pleased, didn't they? They've been planning this for about a year. I think they planned it since first day you moved into the house next door to theirs. For some reason, you impressed my parents."

"Don't you feel manipulated, Josh?" Beth asked and looked at the man as he drove the car through the Los Angeles streets.

"Perhaps, but I'm rather enjoying it. My parents can manipulate me into dating any time they want when it's with a beautiful young lady who has the prettiest eyes I've ever seen. You see, Beth, my parents and your parents and I all agree that you and I dating is a good thing. Now all I have to do is convince my pretty date that it's a good thing and we'll all be happy," Josh remarked as he smiled at his date.

"You don't even know me. I may have a terrible temper. I may throw things. I could be a terrible nagger. How can you even think about going along with our parents when you don't know me?" Beth asked.

"But I do know a lot about you, Beth. You can't imagine all

the things that my parents have written about you. Some things you probably don't want me to know. I even know when you broke up with the last fellow you went with a few months ago. I believe his name was John Davis, right?"

Beth could feel the color rise in her face. She was angry and wanted to laugh at the same time. It was one thing for the Sweenys to plan for their son to date her, but quite another thing for her parents to try to marry her off—especially to an Alaskan.

"You're speechless?" asked her date with a "gotcha" in his voice.

"I'm trying hard to take this in the right way. I'm just a little angry but also amused that my parents would tell so much about my private life. Actually, if you must know, John Davis was only a friend. There was nothing serious, at least on my part. When he got too interested, that's when the parting came. I am only twenty-four, hardly an old maid yet even though my parents may fear that fate is waiting for me. I just graduated from college and was about to look for work. I'm certainly not ready to settle down to married life without living a little first. I've watched my friends marry too quickly and too young. I'm not all that sure that they are as happy about their situations as they thought they would be." Beth's words were a little harsh.

"Can we call a truce, Beth?" Josh asked. He felt that he was getting off on the wrong foot with this girl and that was not what he wanted. "Perhaps our parents are pushing us together, but what do you say that we just enjoy the next three weeks and let them push. It will please all four of our parents. If we're both paranoid about being pushed as a couple, we won't enjoy each other's company. Truce?"

"Truce!"

Chapter 3

The Proposal

The truce was working. Although they hadn't planned to spend every evening together, that's what happened. Beth and Josh discovered someplace that they wanted to go together each evening. Sometimes the parents were included and other times they went alone. Beth took him to all the fascinating places she had visited since coming to Los Angeles. At the end of the first week, they were beginning to be very close friends.

On the first day of the second week of Josh's visit, he took Beth to an exclusive restaurant where the two enjoyed a lobster dinner. Afterwards, the young man took his date down to the pier where the two watched the boats coming and going. They held hands as they walked along the sand on the beach. Beth took off her shoes and socks to walk barefooted in the sand, so Josh did the same. She was thinking how the warm sunny evening produced such a relaxing feeling. Just down the beach was a big rock and Beth and Josh raced to see who reached the rock first. Beth didn't have a chance except she grabbed Josh's shirt and hung on. Laughing, the two sat down on the rock to talk and watch the sun go down and the moon rise although neither of them did much talking.

Finally, Josh put his arms around Beth and pulled her close to him. This young woman meant more to him than he had admitted to himself.

"I know I did a little teasing when I first met you, Beth. But now I'm so much in love with you that I don't know if I can live without you. I didn't plan this. I was only trying to please my parents by dating you and having a good time. But I love you very much." Josh moved toward Beth and she didn't move away. Holding her close, Josh kissed her tenderly at first and then again more firmly as if to let her feel his love.

Beth caught her breath and thought of what he had said. This had been a fascinating week and she too felt that she was falling in love. How could one fall in love in one week? But this man was exactly what she wanted. Tall, good looking, well mannered, tender, caring—she could keep going on. Only, he was an Alaskan. Josh had talked so much about Alaska that she almost thought she might like to go there for a visit. In fact, the more he talked the more fascinated she was with the state of Alaska.

When Beth was quiet and didn't say anything, Josh whispered, "Is it too soon to ask you to marry me, Elizabeth Vandermeer?" Joshua Sweeny held his breath. He almost couldn't believe what he was saying—but he was in love.

Beth cuddled closer in his arms and looked up directly into his deep blue eyes. "Have we known each other only one week? It seems that I've known you always and forever. Oh, Josh, I do love you. This has been such a special week spending every day with you. Yes, I'll marry you," she whispered.

"I can't go back to Alaska without you? Will you marry me in the next two weeks and go back with me?"

"Yes," she said leaving no doubt about how she felt. "When I marry you will that make me an adopted Alaskan? Do you think I'll like Alaska and can adjust to living there? I've heard it gets very cold."

"You will love it, Darling. And, Alaska will love you. There are so many things there I want to show you and teach you about Alaska. You can help me finish our home and make it a real beautiful place. With your touches, it will be a beautiful place to live. Oh, Beth, I never thought I could love anyone as much as I love you!"

"What if I can't adjust to the cold? What if ..."

"We don't want to play what if games, Beth. I love you and you love me. We'll make this a very special marriage and no matter where we live, we'll be happy. But I know you'll like the adventures you'll have in Alaska. I just know it!" Josh was tenderly caressing her face and looking deep in her eyes.

"What do you think our parents will say?" Beth asked.

"Mine will want to celebrate and I have an idea yours will too. They thought neither one of us were ever going to marry, at least not on our own," Josh commented. "I think my folks had about given up on me."

"I'm sure Mom and Dad will be happy to have you for a son-in-law and also to have an excuse to visit Alaska. I can't believe that I'm actually going to live there," Beth mused. "I'm really not a pioneer type, you know."

"You don't have to be a pioneer. We have all the comforts you have here—believe me, Beth. Pioneering in Alaska was a lot harder than my easy life. It's just that Alaska has everything I ever wanted in scenic views, fishing, hunting, skiing, friends, you name it and Alaska has it."

"Have your parents ever been up to Alaska to visit you?"

"Yes, they have and they love it up there. However, Dad's job is down here in Los Angels and he can't leave at this time. They talked about moving after he retired, but that's some time off yet and I don't think they will want to move as they get older. They've lived in their house too long to walk away from it. They were living there when I was born. I think they'll just talk about it and enjoy thinking about moving to Alaska, but I don't think they ever will," Josh remarked.

"When I first saw you and heard about you, I sure didn't want anything to do with Alaska, but you've convinced me that it is a different place than I thought it was. I'm anxious to see it now. I plan on enjoying it."

"Oh, yes you'll enjoy Alaska, you can count on that. I've watched your face as I related some of my experiences to you. You were fascinated. You'll be a great Alaska partner. And, really, we are fully civilized up there. I have a nice home even if it isn't quite finished. It isn't a pioneer's life at all, I promise," Josh reemphasized. He stopped to let her take in all the things he had been talking about. Joshua Sweeny had met so many people that believed that Alaskans lived in igloos and had nothing as far as convenience was concerned. Most people had to go there to see that Alaska was like anyplace else, only better in his opinion.

Then Josh decided it was time to make some plans. "How soon can we get married, Darling? I want you to go back to Alaska with me. After meeting you and being with you for just one week, I can't imagine life without you. You know, Beth, I thought I would marry some day, I just never thought I would fall in love so hard. I'm not sure I believed in love until I met you. I thought I would marry someone I was rather fond of and we'd have a family. Never did I think I could love someone as much as I love you."

Josh started smiling. "My friends in Alaska are going to be shocked. They call me the resident bachelor. I'm so anxious to introduce you to them. They'll welcome you with open arms—after the initial shock."

"All your girl friends too?" she asked.

"All of them," he smirked. Then for the third time, he said, "Beth, I want you to go back with me in two weeks. Is that asking too much too soon?"

Beth gasped a little with excitement. "If we're going to get married within the next two weeks, we'd better start making some plans. I've made friends at the university that I'd like to invite and some neighbors. What about you, Josh? How many people do you know around here?"

"A good many," Josh replied. "I've lived here all my life until I moved up north. I just went up there with an uncle for a vacation and never moved back home. I've been up there for ten years now."

"That means you moved up there when you were … ?"

"Nineteen," Josh grinned. "It might be good if you knew a few statistics about your future husband. I'm twenty-nine, Beth. Now you see why my parents felt that I would never marry. To tell you the truth, Beth, I was having too much fun in Alaska to even think about getting married. I'm like you, I've watched some of my friends marry and then most of the adventure leaves. Kids come along and they settle down to 'old married people.' And maybe that's the way it's supposed to be. I just never met anyone I wanted to settle down with before I met you."

Josh pulled her close again and kissed her. Beth felt that it didn't matter if he was an Alaskan or if they lived in the Arctic, as long as she could be with Josh, she would be happy.

The next evening, the couple invited both sets of parents out to dinner. They had told them that there were some things to talk over. Both Jean and Sarah smiled to themselves. They were sure they knew exactly what the two wanted to discuss.

After they were seated in the restaurant, they glanced at the menus. The waitress, whose nametag read Sharon, came by and took their orders. She smiled at Beth and Josh. The waitress was thinking about what Josh had told her earlier and wanted to watch him when he made his presentation to the parents.

Josh began talking about Alaska. He knew the Vandermeers were intrigued with his Alaskan stories. Soon he looked up and noticed the waitress waiting for his nod to deliver the dinner. Finally, he managed to get up enough nerve to stand up and with his knife he carefully hit his drinking glass to call everyone to attention.

"I have an announcement to make," he said nervously.

Beth looked at him and smiled to herself. Never did she think he would ever be nervous about anything. He was so big and burley and able to lick anything, but timid about telling his parents and soon to be parents-in-law about the upcoming marriage. Beth was amused.

"Ah ... you see, Beth and I ... we plan on getting married real soon," he said and sat down.

Beth burst out laughing as Josh glared at her. "I'm sorry, Josh, but I just never knew you could be nervous," she whispered. "Now that wasn't really that hard to say, was it?"

"It was terrible! But now that it's over, what do you parents think about it?" Josh asked.

"Great!" was the reply from all four parents. Mr. Vandermeer was the first to comment further. "I couldn't give my daughter to anyone else and be this happy about it. I know she loves you, Josh, and I know you'll make her happy. I don't know if you can make an Alaskan out of her, though. She loves sunny California."

"She'll love Alaska. It gets very warm in the summer time and we can always visit here in the winter and warm up a little. We want to get married within the next two weeks," Josh said anxiously.

"Fine," said Jean Vandermeer. "We'll all work together and get it planned. My daughter has always said she didn't want a big affair if she ever did get married. If she still holds that view, we ought to be able to get everything done in a week. The dress will be the first thing we must look for."

Josh waved to the waitress to bring their meal. He had asked her not to deliver the meal until he motioned to her. She was a friend of his and he told her what he was planning to do and didn't want interrupted until it was over with.

"Now," said Matthew Vandermeer, "I think we should eat our dinner and we can finish the wedding planning at home. Just make sure that cabin of yours has room for visitors this next summer because we'll be coming up."

Beth watched as the two mothers talked—they were so excited. They couldn't have been more pleased about the upcoming marriage. Each had their own ideas what they should do and how they could get it all done in a week. Beth really didn't care. She just wanted to get married and be with Josh.

Josh and Beth were eating while the others were making plans. They were finished and had to wait for the other four to stop talking and start eating.

After the meal, the parents left the potential bride and groom alone and headed back home. When the waitress came by, Josh paid her.

"By the smile that is on your face, I assume that everything went like you wanted it to, right?" Sharon asked.

"It went just fine," Beth said, "especially after this nervous man worked up enough nerve to stand up and announce our wedding." Beth was laughing.

"You have to be kidding. Josh has never been shy or nervous. You mean that he had trouble making this simple announcement? I can't believe it," Sharon exclaimed and the two ladies laughed.

When they left the restaurant, Josh explained that he had known Sharon for years and had been best man at her and Dave's wedding. "If Sharon gets half a chance to give me a bad time, that's just what she'll do. When I think about the bad time I gave her at her wedding, maybe she has a reason for revenge."

"What did you do?" Beth asked frowning.

"Oh, you know the usual."

Beth decided that she didn't even want to know what the usual was.

The evening was over and Beth was lying in bed thinking things over. In one week her whole life and her plans for her life had changed. But, she was happy—very happy. Just to be with Josh was all she wanted now. She had planned on getting a job at the local hospital since she had a degree in nursing, but there would be nursing jobs in Alaska and she could go to work there.

Chapter 4

The Wedding Day

Both mothers and Beth drove to the big mall where they knew there was a wedding shop. Beth wasn't completely at ease with her future mother-in-law coming along, but since her mother invited Sarah Sweeny, the prospective bride would have to make the best of it.

Jean drove straight to the wedding shop and parked the car. The three walked into the shop and looked around. It was definitely the place to look for wedding needs. Not only were there plenty of wedding dresses displayed, there were veils, wedding slippers, garters, and everything one would need to complete the wedding ensemble. Beth went from one wedding dress to another carefully examining each one. When she had seen all the gowns displayed, Beth frowned.

"Is this all you have? I had something a little different in mind," she said disappointingly. Beth explained to the saleslady exactly the type of gown she was looking for including the details concerning the sleeves and the neck design and the waist along with the dress length.

"Miss Vandermeer, we do have a gown almost exactly like what you described. However, it's a gown that someone took home and then returned it. The girl changed her mind and decided she couldn't afford it. I really don't know if she wore it or not. Would you like to see it even though it might be second hand? It doesn't appear to be damaged in any way."

"Oh, yes, I definitely would like to see it," she exclaimed excitingly. It would be nice if she could find the dress she wanted, second hand or not.

"Just wait here and I'll be right back," the clerk said as she hurried to the back of the store and through the door. In a minute she was right back with the dress, holding it up for Beth to view.

"Oh, oh, that's just perfect. I love it. Did you make sure there were no tears or stains?"

"I only briefly examined it. Why don't we examine it more thoroughly together?" she asked laying the gown carefully on the table while the three ladies searched the gown for spots. "It doesn't appear hurt in anyway stains. Is it the right size for you? It sure looks as though it would fit you," the clerk declared.

"I'll try it on," Beth replied eagerly.

When she came out of the dressing room, the three women were excited. "It's a perfect fit, Beth, and you look positively beautiful in it," declared her mother, and the clerk and Sarah Sweeny agreed.

"Well, Mom, that's one thing off our list. This is the gown I was hoping to find. Now we have to find a florist and order some flowers for the church and for the attendants."

"Oh, no, Beth, the ladies from the church want to furnish the flowers for the decoration and Josh and his father will purchase your bouquet along with flowers for the attendants," reported her future mother-in-law.

"Oh, then that's another thing we can cross off the list. Now we have to buy the food for the reception after we plan the meal."

"Oh, no, Beth, you needn't worry about that either," Mrs. Sweeny exclaimed. "I talked to a lady in the church and she said the ladies wanted to furnish the meal for the reception if you would tell them what you would like to have. They really do like Josh and want to do all they can to help him with the wedding."

"That's really nice of them, Sarah. It takes a load off my mind. Now, I guess shoes and a veil is all I have left to buy or Mom can I use your veil. I always loved the way that veil was designed. I don't think I could buy one I would like any better."

"I'd be pleased and honored if you wore my wedding veil, Beth. Since you and I wear the same shoes, I have a pair of white slippers I wore to a formal dinner. I only wore them once. Why don't you try them on?"

"You do have some good ideas, Mom. I remember the slippers and they are exactly what I wanted."

The shoppers returned home. Beth could hardly wait until she could wear the dress down the aisle to meet Josh. She knew the dress really complimented her. She felt like a bride when she put it on in the wedding shop. When she mentioned showing the gown to Josh this evening, both women absolutely forbid her. "He can't see the gown until you walk down the aisle," her mother declared and Sarah Sweeny agreed.

After several days, Beth suddenly remembered that she had to buy a ring for Josh. Why didn't she remember that? How embarrassing it would be if she was at the wedding and the minister asked her to put the ring on Josh's finger and she wouldn't have one. How could she forget an important detail like that? Everything else had worked out so well, now she needed to find a ring.

"Mom, why didn't we remember that I needed a ring for Josh? I have to find out Josh's ring size. I'll give him a call."

Beth picked up the phone and dialed the Sweeny home. Josh answered. "I have to get you a ring and I don't know your size?"

"Beth, I found matching rings for both of us. I brought it home for you to see. I'll be right over to show you," declared the groom-to-be.

Josh walked into the house and displayed the rings. "They are beautiful, Josh. I love them. But I'm supposed to pay for your ring."

"Who made that dumb rule?"

"Josh, you know that's the way it is. You buy my ring and I buy yours."

"It's already bought and paid for because I knew you would like them. The jeweler did say I could return them if you didn't care for them."

"But you can't pay for your own wedding ring. It just isn't done."

"So, sue me."

Beth ignored Josh's remark since she knew she had lost the argument. The prospective bride exclaimed, "I think we're all ready for the wedding. Mom's making the wedding cake and your church is furnishing the reception. I have my wedding dress and you have the rings. The bridesmaids have their dresses and I assume your attendants have their tuxes. We forgot about the flower girl and ring bearer? Oh dear, what will we do about that. Maybe we won't need to have any, although the flower girl and ring bearer are always a neat part in a wedding."

"There's a girl and boy from the church who volunteered and I said yes, since I didn't think you had anyone in mind. One of the bridesmaids made a dress for Carrie and we rented a tux for Sammy. I forgot to tell you. Did I make a mistake?" Josh asked.

"No, that's great. I'm glad you asked them. It appears we're all set." Beth walked over and hugged her prospective bridegroom. "Day after tomorrow is our wedding day. I can't believe it. I'm actually getting married."

"You can't believe you're getting married. I can't believe that I am getting married. We're a pair, Beth," he said and kissed his prospective bride on the cheek.

On the day of the wedding, the participants were hurrying around here and there checking to see if all was done that needed to be done. The ceremony would begin at ten in the morning and the meal would be planned for twelve o'clock. Sometime in the afternoon the bride and groom would leave for their honeymoon.

As she entered the church, Beth was pleased. The flowers and decorations were just the way she wanted them. The color schemes blended with the attendants' dresses and complimented the whole wedding scene. Beth was excited that in one week they were able to pull off such a beautiful wedding.

When the bride walked down the aisle escorted by her dad, Josh looked up and smiled. Beth was beautiful, he thought, very beautiful.

A friend of the Sweeny family sang a love song for the two. The minister gave a quick sermon on how to make their marriage successful. Elizabeth Vandermeer was thrilled with the ceremony and all of the things that the minister had said. When he finally asked her if she would take this man as her husband, she rang out loud and clear, "I will."

Josh rang out his "I will" loud and clear with a big smile on his face. The two exchanged the exquisite rings Josh had purchased. When it was all over the newlyweds walked quickly back down the aisle and out the church where birdseed flew in every direction. They walked over to the church hall smiling and covered with birdseed. As they entered the large room where the reception was being held, the two were so happy they smiled all the way through the reception.

Since the bride and groom had plenty of time before the meal, they opened all their gifts. Josh looked at the big pile of gifts wondering how he would ever get them up to Alaska. Dan Sweeny read his son's thoughts. "Don't worry, Son, I'll ship these up to you. It will be much easier that way." Josh agreed.

As they were about to leave, two of Josh's friends came over and said they needed to borrow the bride for a minute. Josh stood up tall, towering over the two and said, "Lay one hand on my wife and you'll sleep till morning." The two decided not to abduct the bride and settled for decorating the car.

After the meal was finished, the bride and groom were on their way to their honeymoon suite in a non-disclosed location. Josh made sure he lost the car that had been trailing him ever since he drove away from the church. Those two jokers who planned on kidnapping his bride were not giving up easily. Josh made a few twists and turns on the road and drove into an underground parking lot and waited for some time. He and Beth were laughing because they had finally ditched the two friends that were following them. When Josh was sure he was safe from the trailing car, he drove back out of the parking lot and on the street and headed for the motel the two had selected.

The couple honeymooned at the various sites in California and came back to spend the last couple of days with the parents before their departure to Alaska.

Beth had a few moments with her mom alone while Josh and her dad were talking on the porch.

"Darling, do you think you'll be very lonely for us? I'm a little worried because you are going so far away. I hope you'll be so happy, that you won't miss your home and us that much," Jean said.

"Don't forget, Mom, I spent four years at college. I'm used to being away. I knew I could always come home then when I wanted so this will be different. But I'll make it. I love Josh so very much I know we'll be happy. It'll be different in Alaska. Very different! From some of the things that Josh tells me, I know I have to make adjustments. But everyone has to make adjustments once they are married. Mom, he's so kind and tender. Don't worry about us. We'll be fine."

"There is always the telephone," Jean reminded her daughter. "You can call us anytime you want. It's hard to believe that you'll be gone tomorrow. But you remember to call us, won't you?"

"Yes, Mom, I'll be calling. Probably run up a big bill the first year. You must come up when Dad gets a vacation from work."

The next morning the parents and newlyweds headed for the airport. Beth was so excited about the whole journey and living in Alaska, she could hardly eat. Josh had filled her so full of neat tales of his beloved state, Beth could hardly wait for the plane to land on Alaska territory.

It was the end of January. February would be here in a few days. That's when the weather usually starts warming up in most places. Back east, after the long cold winter, things would begin to warm up in March, but in Los Angeles, it never did get cold. How different Alaska would be! When she did get to Alaska, Beth assumed that spring should be right around the corner.

Chapter 5

Arriving in Alaska

The further north the airplane took them, the cooler the weather got. Beth looked out the window and noticed the mountains of snow they were passing. It didn't look remotely close to spring as far as she could see. It was only a couple more hours and they would be at the Fairbanks Airport. Did she hear the pilot correctly? He said it was 40 degrees below. He must have meant 40 degrees. This time of year, it couldn't possibly be 40 degrees below.

Finally the plane landed and they prepared to enter the airport. A cold chill ran over her. It was cold here, colder than 40 degrees. On the way out, she asked the stewardess how cold it was. "Only forty below," was the answer.

Beth tried not to look surprised. Josh had told her to put in her warmest coat and boots. Now she was glad she did although Los Angeles coats and boots were quite different than what she was seeing the Alaskans wearing. As soon as she reached the airport, she told her new husband that she wanted to go to the lady's room and put on warmer clothes. Josh had insisted that she carry some warmer clothes in her backpack if she didn't want to wear them on the plane. She smiled and agreed that it would be a good idea although she was perfectly comfortable with what she was wearing. Beth had an extra sweater in her backpack and another pair of socks that should help. She had put in a pair of Capri pants in her backpack and quickly slipped them on under her slacks. That should do it, she thought.

Josh headed for the baggage area and found his friends, Lonnie and Candice Adams, waiting for him.

"How was your vacation?" he asked.

"It was great and I brought back a surprise for you both. I'm quite sure that Candice will especially enjoy this surprise."

"Where is the surprise," Candice asked.

"Be here in a minute. Be patient, Candice."

Josh was pulling his luggage off the belt as it came close to him. The two friends watched as he pulled six suitcases off the baggage belt. "That's all the baggage I brought," Josh stated.

"In which suitcase is the surprise?" asked an anxious Candice. She loved surprises and couldn't wait to see what Josh brought back from Los Angeles.

"It's not here yet, Candice."

"Didn't you say that this was all of the luggage you brought with you when you pulled them off the belt? Now where's the surprise?"

"This surprise doesn't come by way of luggage, Miss Curiosity."

Candice shook her head. "That's a lot of luggage for one person. How'd you talk them into letting you bring all this? Must have cost you a bundle, huh? What all did you bring back, anyway? Just what have you got in those bags?" asked an impatient and curious Candice.

Josh looked up to see Beth heading his way. He smiled at her and walked over to her and put his arms around his new wife.

"This is what I brought back to answer your first question. You'll have to ask my wife, Beth, what's in her luggage—that is if you really want to know."

Candice and Lonnie's mouths dropped open. This confirmed bachelor was now married. They didn't know what to say and they just stared at the beautiful girl that Josh said was his wife.

"That was fast work old man," was all that Lonnie managed to say. Candice was unable to speak.

Finally, Lonnie realized how unwelcoming and impolite the two had been to the newcomer. "I'm sorry," he said to Beth. My name is Lonnie and this is my wife, Candice. We are so glad to meet you, Mrs. Sweeny. Pardon us for being so rude, but we are shocked. Josh here has always been 'our confirmed resident bachelor.' We've been trying for years to match him up with some of the girls around here, but didn't have any luck. But now I see he didn't need any help from us. It appears he's done a pretty good job picking out his own wife."

"My name is Elizabeth, but everyone calls me Beth. It's nice to meet both of you. I've never been to Alaska before and I'm very glad to make acquaintance with my husband's friends. Do you live close to Josh?" she asked.

"We're practically neighbors. Not all that far from him. You might as well know that I plan on visiting you a lot," smiled Candice. "Oh, we're going to have such a good time together and I just know we're going to be very good friends." Candice walked over to Beth and linked her arm with Beth's. "Those fellows can take care of the luggage. Let's go get a cup of coffee and have a good talk while they get the luggage into the car and get it warmed up. You don't need to go out into a cold car on your first trip here. Not at forty-two below."

"I thought it was just forty below," mumbled Beth and laughed. "It's hard to think about forty below when I just came from eighty degree weather. This will take some time to get used to. I really thought the captain made a mistake when he said Fairbanks weather was forty below."

Candice and Beth were right in the middle of their conversation when the men joined them. The two had a cup of coffee with the ladies before heading for the automobile that was warming up.

When Beth stepped out into the cold almost anticipating the experience, it took her breath away. It wasn't long before she felt that her eyeballs were freezing. Josh put his arm around her and whispered, "Don't take deep breaths. Just keep your head down and I'll guide you to the car."

Beth couldn't remember ever being so cold. When Josh said something about long johns, she had laughed. When he suggested heavier slacks, she turned up her nose. They would look so ugly. She wasn't about to wear long johns and ugly slacks. Tomorrow, she would purchase several pairs of long johns and look for some wool slacks. The cold went right through her slacks even though it was a short distance to the car.

As they drove through the town of Fairbanks, Beth was fascinated with the snow-lined trees and bushes which appeared to have crystals hanging on them. Everything looked like a beautiful painting. "This is gorgeous, Josh. I've never seen anything so beautiful. It reminds me of the winter wonderland song."

"The snow freezes on the bushes and trees throughout the winter. There are crystals in the air and that's called ice fog. It's a beautiful sight to see. I've painted a few pictures like this for our home," he stated.

Painted, thought Beth, he paints? Wonder what else I'll find out about my new husband that I barely know.

Turning to Lonnie, Josh asked, "How are things at my house now? Did the pipes freeze or any trouble with anything? I trust that it did survive the cold and my house is ready for me to bring my bride home."

"Yes, I think you finally have things wrapped enough so they won't freeze. We built a fire and made sure all the water faucets worked. It should be nice and cozy for this Californian who has to learn to dress Alaskan style," Lonnie remarked.

"Are you all right, Beth?" Candice asked. "You look so cold."

"Now that I'm in the car, I feel much better," she answered.

"We discussed some extra clothing and she turned her nose up, but I figured by tomorrow, we would pick up some warmer things and Beth would be more agreeable," Josh grinned.

"You got that right," said the new wife. "I want one of those coats like Candice has."

"I thought you said they were ugly when I showed them to you in the catalogue," he reminded his wife with a twinkle in his eyes.

"I've changed my mind," she grinned. "Women are allowed to change their minds. Isn't that right, Candice?"

"It sure is and these men better remember that," she agreed.

"You'll have a parka tomorrow, Mrs. Sweeny," promised her husband. "If you dress properly, you'll be surprised how quickly you can adapt to the cold. A warm parka, gloves, lined boots, warm scarf, wool pants and some long johns and you'll be ready for the fifty below weather they predicted was coming this next week."

Beth stared wide-eyed at her husband. Hopefully, he was just joking. Fifty below? No way. But then, it was already forty-two below. Maybe he wasn't joking.

As they drove up to her new home, Beth surveyed the area. The setting was wonderful. All those trees framed the big log house and looked so inviting. They reminded her of Christmas trees lined with white decorations and imitation snow. She had never seen a house like the one she was about to enter. It fascinated her. He said he had a nice house and now she believed him. If the inside was as great as the outside, she would be more than pleased.

"How far are we from Fairbanks?"

"About 20 miles," Josh answered.

Lonnie and Candice followed them into the house. Lonnie was right. It was nice and warm when she walked in. She noticed a wood stove in the spacious living room. Beth kept her wits about her as she glanced around the room. It was spacious all right, but it was obviously decorated by a man. She would gradually put some feminine touches here and there and she wouldn't wait too long to do it.

"How is it you have such a big place, Josh?" Beth asked. "I thought you said you had a log cabin in the wilderness."

"It's a log cabin. I started small and kept building. In spite of what everyone believed, I knew some day I would fall in love, get married and would need a house that could take care of a dozen or so kids." Josh never batted an eye.

"Planning on adopting some, huh?" asked the new wife which brought a roar of laughter from their company.

"Glad to see you can hold your own, Beth. You're going to find out that you'll need a sense of humor if you're going to put up with this guy. Well, we really should be going and let you two settle in. Why don't you come over tomorrow and we'll have dinner together?" Lonnie suggested.

"We'll do that," replied Beth before her husband had a chance to reply. She liked Candice from the start and wanted to get more acquainted. "Just where do you live from here?"

"Just about half a mile down the road," Candice answered. "It'll be a good walk in the summer time."

"I thought you said you were neighbors?"

"We are the closest neighbors Josh has."

"Oh." Her neighbors at home lived 20 feet away. Beth couldn't imagine the closest neighbor being one-half mile away. Things were different in Alaska, all right!

Lonnie spoke up as he and Candice walked towards the door. "Just bring your Cheechako over to our house tomorrow and we'll acquaint her with a little Alaskan living. We'll try to initiate her into Alaska."

"What did he mean by the crack ... Chee ... ?"

"It just means you're a newcomer to Alaska. He's trying to get your dandruff up."

"If I had any, it would have worked," she said and laughed. So she was a Chee something. Okay. She was new in Alaska. It was just that Lonnie said it in a derogatory manner. Beth wasn't too sure but that the two of them made up the word.

After their "neighbors" left and the newlyweds were alone in the big house, Josh took her through the whole house including the attic that would some day be an upstairs with bedrooms.

"I don't see any vents for heat," Beth stated.

"I just use the wood stove. It works great and it will keep you warm."

"All night long?"

"All night. It's an airtight stove and just a log will burn the whole night. You wait and see."

"Is the cooking stove gas?"

"It's propane."

"Oh. It is a nice big house. You won't mind if I make it a little more feminine, will you?"

"I'm expecting you to. My mother gave me a big lecture about letting you buy what you need to make it suit you. I didn't think I needed the lecture, but perhaps it made me understand that women think a little differently than men. Mom said that the way the house looked was very important to a woman. I took her word for it. Tomorrow we'll go shopping not only for warmer clothes and especially long johns," he grinned, "but also for anything else you think you might want to start making this your home."

Josh looked at her tenderly. "I'm so glad that you're here, Sweetheart. I love you so very much. How did I ever live without you?" He brought his bride closer to him and kissed her and the two tired travelers retired for the evening.

Chapter 6

Take Off Your Shoes

"It is warm in here," Beth remarked to herself as she hopped out of bed the next morning. It was hard to believe that a wood stove could warm a whole house. Josh must have slipped out of bed earlier, as he was not in the room. She could smell the coffee brewing when she entered the kitchen.

As she glanced around, Beth couldn't see Josh anywhere. Where could he be? The wife poured a cup of coffee for herself and sat down on the stool by the counter. She slowly sipped the hot coffee. It was good. "Wonder what brand he uses? I wonder if he can cook as good as he makes coffee," she thought. Finally, she arose and walked around the house noticing the pictures positioned on the wall. All at once she gasped. There was a picture of her framed in an expensive frame and displayed as if it were the center of attraction. That was a picture she had given her mother!

Mother must have given this picture to Josh's mother who sent it on to Josh. No wonder he felt as though he knew her. He'd been staring at her picture for six months. Both of their parents did a pretty good job of matchmaking. But she had to admit that she readily approved. There wasn't another man she ever met that was like Josh.

She was still holding her picture when Josh came through the arctic entrance and on into the house.

"What are you doing with my picture? That kept me warm just looking at it all through this winter," he said with a grin.

"Our parents were determined, weren't they?"

"Mine were at least. I don't know if you'll believe this or not, but I think I fell in love with the picture first. I kept telling myself that you would disappoint me when I met you, but I loved you before I even saw you in person," confessed the husband.

"I have to admit that I did study your pictures at your Mom's. And believe me there were enough of them scattered around the living room and on the walls. I don't know how many she had in the bedrooms, as I never ventured into any room except the living room and the kitchen. She did ask me if I wanted one of your pictures, but I told her no, that she should keep them. I thought it was cute of her, never dreaming that my mother gave her one to send to you. But I have to admit that I'm glad they arranged the matchmaking which resulted in our marriage," Beth giggled.

"Me, too," Josh admitted. "Now, I ran out and got some things for breakfast, as I didn't have much here. Do you want a big breakfast or just sweet rolls and juice? What do you usually have?"

"I usually just have toast and coffee, but I'm starved this morning. Here, let me fry some bacon and eggs and you can make some toast. Let's start this out right with a good healthy breakfast. What are we going to do after that?" she asked.

"Well, I only have four more days and I have to go back to work. We're going shopping today to get all the things we mentioned yesterday. Also, you need an Alaskan driver's license. I'll get you a book and you can peruse it to see if you need to study or not." Josh paused. "Did you really want to go to work, Beth? You don't have to, but if you do, I'll understand."

"I would like to work part time. Hospitals usually have a lot of part time nurses. I think I would get bored in the wintertime if I didn't. But if you only have one car, how will I get to the work place?" she asked.

"I have two vehicles. And, then our schedules could coincide. I can keep the type of hours I need. I have a very flexible work schedule. As long as I get the work done, my boss doesn't care where I accomplish it."

"Josh, what do you do for a living?"

"I'm an engineer."

"It's always good for a wife to know that in case someone asks," she smiled. There was a lot about this man that she didn't know and needed to find out.

"Josh, what is that funny little entrance way we came through to get into the house? It doesn't seem to do anything as far as the looks of the house."

"That, my dear, is an arctic entrance. When you open the door in the winter the cold air only comes in that far and not all through the house. You noticed the coats and boot and shoe racks. Most Alaskans remove the outdoor shoes and wear slippers or socks to keep the carpets neat."

Beth quickly looked down at her shoes and the carpet.

Josh smiled. "Don't worry about this carpet. I deliberately got a multicolored dark carpet that wouldn't show the dirt. I didn't want to stop and take off my shoes every time I came into the house. If you wish to change the carpet later, we'll talk about that. But for now don't worry about it. But be prepared to take off your shoes when we visit Candice. It's just an Alaska custom for people who like clean houses and carpets. We don't have nice sidewalks to walk on up here and you drag in a lot of dirt and sand that isn't any too good for carpets. Makes them look ugly and wear out faster."

Beth nodded her head. Here she had been in Alaska for only few hours and had learned so much, but she had a feeling there was a lot more learning to do.

"Before we go shopping, I have something for you." Josh walked into the bedroom and came out holding a pair of long johns. "My mom wore these when she came up to visit. I thought you might like to use these today even if the long johns are a little big for you. The thermometer reads 45 degrees below. That's colder than it has been. When we buy the right size at the store, you can change into them if it will make you more comfortable."

Beth grabbed the long johns. She shivered at the thought of 45 degrees below zero and willingly put on the winter clothing. "Thank you. I'm sure these will be an improvement over what I wore last night. I thought my legs were going to freeze just walking to the car. I've never been so cold in my life. I remembered what you said in LA and thought I should have followed your advice."

Smiling, Josh left to start the car so it would be nice and warm for his bride. He wondered if Beth was going to have to learn everything the hard way. He had talked hard before leaving LA trying to get her to buy long johns and heavier slacks, but no way could he talk her into it. Now she was happy to put on a pair of oversized long johns. He shook his head. He would let her learn in her own way. Josh had to admit that they were both strong-minded and had to learn things for themselves. He could remember back when he learned a few things the hard way. They were a pair, he and his wife.

Beth came out to the garage in a few minutes and looked around. It wasn't as cold in the garage as she thought it should be. "How come the garage is warm, Josh?" she asked.

"It's a heated garage. If we didn't have that we would be getting into a very cold car every day. Lots of Alaskans have heated garages. It does make life a lot nicer to get into a car that's been in a heated garage rather than one that has set out all night in 45 degrees below weather."

"I'll agree with that. I expected it to be cold."

Beth walked around the front of the car to get to the passenger side. She stopped and had a puzzled look on her face as she stared at the front of the car. She looked up at Josh and asked, "Why on earth do you have an electric plug in the front of your car? Is this an electric car or something? I didn't think they had electric cars this big."

"It's an electric car all right and you should see the long electric cord I have to have to get clear to Fairbanks," he said with his wicked grin.

"I know better than that," she snapped.

"Beth, all cars up here have plugs in the front of them. You plug the car in at night to keep the oil warmed up so the car starts easily and you plug them in when you are shopping when it gets cold out. Then you can start the car up easily. Does that make any sense to you?"

"Yeah, I guess it does. This is certainly a different country with different ways. I feel like a kindergarten child just learning about life," remarked the wife as she climbed into the vehicle, "or perhaps a foreigner in this country trying to figure out a new way of life and a new language." She was wearing a parka that Josh's mother wore when she visited. It was a little large but she was much warmer compared to yesterday's experience even though it was colder out today.

The trip to town proved to be fascinating to Beth. The newcomer was surprised to find most her favorite stores in Fairbanks. Beth was pleased. Although Los Angeles had a large selection of shops and department stores, Beth rarely shopped anywhere except in her three favorite stores. The town of Fairbanks wasn't so different from the town she lived in back east, but it certainly was different than Los Angeles.

By noon, Beth had pretty well finished her shopping and the two had lunch at the Chinese Restaurant. It tasted good to her. Why had she thought Fairbanks would have no decent place to eat? There were multiple restaurants to choose from. The new Alaskan had decided that sooner or later she would try them all. When the shopping spree was over, the car was packed with clothes and household furnishings.

One thing that Beth didn't do while she was in town was look for work. She had decided to wait for a while until she was accustomed to the house and the weather. She realized there was no hurry in finding a job when she accidentally ran across one of her husband's pay slips as well as his bank statement. Josh had explained before that the house was totally paid for as he had built it and paid cash for the materials needed. Finances would not be one of their problems.

When Josh handed her a driver's handbook, she glanced through it and decided that she could pass the test. Most of the questions were about the same as California or other states. They headed for the Department of Motor Vehicles and shortly afterwards, Beth walked out of the building with an Alaskan driver's license. She held her paper up to her husband showing him her score. "I got 100 percent on the written test," she grinned. "Now this should make me a true Alaskan."

"No, actually, you are only a Cheechako," the husband grinned.

"I'm a what?"

"Cheechako."

"That's what Lonnie called me yesterday. Is that really something nice or do you both need your mouth washed out?"

Josh roared with laughter. When he could finally talk, he said, "It just means you are a newcomer to Alaska. You're a tenderfoot. You have to be here for a while before you become a real Alaskan—a sourdough. It takes more than 24 hours, you know. Now, what do you say that we head for home and rest up a bit before we go to Candice and Lonnie's place for dinner?"

"Oh, I had forgotten about that. Yes, let's do that. I want to change into some of my warmer clothes."

The afternoon passed quickly and the couple headed for their friend's home. Candice was all smiles as she welcomed Beth into her home. "It's good to see you again. How did the shopping spree go?"

"Wonderful. I bought enough things to put a little feminine flavor to that home of ours. Josh has given me a free reign, thanks to his mother," laughed Beth. "And, look at my nice warm clothes. My first lesson in Alaska is to dress for the weather. Oh, Candice, I was so cold last night. I was freezing. I sure wished I had listened to Josh when he told me to buy some long johns in California, but I just couldn't bring myself to. But they do feel nice and warm."

"I was raised in this country, so I grew up dressing warmly. But I can imagine what you must think if this is your first time wearing the ugly garments. Just remember that nobody sees them anyway." Dinner was served shortly after Beth and Josh arrived.

Beth was enjoying the roast and vegetables that Candice had served. "Candice, this is one of the best roasts I think I ever ate. It's absolutely delicious with a little different flavor. I was wondering what you put on it."

Josh quickly said, "I'm not sure you should tell her. Let her find out later."

"Why?" asked Candice frowning. "Why shouldn't I tell her?"

"Just wait until the meal is over. I know my wife. Just wait."

Beth put down her fork and stared at both of them. "Is there something wrong with this meat? You all seemed to be eating an ample amount of it. What on earth is it that you don't want to tell me?"

"I just wanted to wait a little while until you knew how good the meat really was, and then I'd tell you about it, but since you're so insistent, I'll tell you now. It's moose meat," Josh explained.

Beth frowned and almost gagged. Moose meat? Ugh. But it tasted so good. She noticed everyone was watching her. Well, she would prove that she was going to make a good Alaskan. She picked up the fork and began eating the meat trying hard not to think of where it came from. Of course roast beef came from cows, so what's the difference? This roast just came from a moose instead. She smiled at them all and kept eating.

Josh patted her on the shoulder. "My little pioneer," he said. "I'm proud of you, Darling. It's pretty good stuff, huh?"

"It really is tasty, Candice. It's just for a minute there it threw me. To think I was eating one of those big ugly animals. I haven't seen one yet, but I'm not too impressed with the pictures I've seen of moose. Do you have a lot of moose up here?" she asked casually hoping the answer was no.

All three of her listeners laughed. "Some," replied Lonnie with a grin. "Just remember that Alaskan animals and everything else are bigger and better than anywhere else in the world." He'd let her find that out for herself how plentiful moose were in Alaska. It's a wonder in the last 24 hours that she hadn't spotted one.

After a pleasant evening chatting and getting acquainted with Candice, Beth was hesitant in heading home. She'd never met anyone before that she felt so close to in such a short time. Beth lingered at the door a few minutes while Candice and she made plans for the day Josh went back to work. "I'll come over and help you feminize that place. I've been dying to do that for years. Even his mom wanted to fix it up a little, but he talked her out of it. I bet she gave him a lecture when he left."

"You're right, she did," butted in Josh. "In no uncertain terms she explained to me how women love to have a 'frilly' house as she put it. You girls just fix it up. I can always go out to my garage when the frills get more than I can take. By the way, ladies, the garage if off-limits when it comes to fixing and feminizing it. There's not going to be any pink curtains out there hanging around my garage windows!" he exclaimed emphatically. Lonnie roared with laughter while Beth and Candice just stared at the two men.

"Beyond hope, Beth, both of them are—way beyond hope. Never mind what they say, we'll fix it so even the men will like it. We won't put pink curtains in the garage, just frilly ones."

With that remark, the Sweenys walked down the driveway to their vehicle. "That was a fun evening," Beth remarked. "They are such nice people. It seems as though I've known them for years instead of just barely 24 hours. I hope we see a lot of them."

"You will, I guarantee it. They love to go fishing as much as I do. Candice is quite the fisher gal. She actually catches more than Lonnie and I do and she makes sure that she tells us so. I can hardly wait to take you fishing, Darling, but that will come in July. We go down to the Kenai Peninsula and stay a week or so. You'll love it."

Beth did everything she could to look interested. She had never been fishing in her life. It just wasn't one of her dad's hobbies. Well, she wouldn't let her new husband know that she'd never been fishing. She would just make the best of it when the time came. How hard could be it? Just throw the line in the water and wait for something to hook it. Josh would fix her line and bait her hook. At least he better help her, as she didn't have any idea how to fix a fishing pole.

Chapter 7

The Aura Borealis

A s the two talked about fishing, Josh suddenly remembered that Beth couldn't go fishing until she purchased a license. "Beth, we must get your fishing license. Let's stop on our way home at the gas station right down the road a ways. They sell fishing licenses and that way you will be all ready when the time comes. There's no telling when that Candice might decide she wants to go fishing and take you with her."

"Sure, that's a good idea," she said trying to put some enthusiasm into her answer.

Beth was back to thinking about the fishing and just how you would go about it. She didn't want to appear too stupid about the whole thing. In ways it sounded fun and in other ways the whole idea made her nervous. There were times when she felt that she was in a whole new country.

"Earth to Beth. Earth to Beth. Come in Beth. Where have you been? What are you thinking about?"

"I'm sorry. I was still thinking about that fishing expedition you were talking about. What were you saying?"

"I was explaining what you could do while I was working. I only have one more day and then I must go back to work. I don't want you to be bored, but it seems our good neighbor plans on coming over and giving you a hand. You and Candice should have a great time together. Why don't we invite them to dinner some night?"

"Good idea. I'll do that."

They stopped at the store and Josh walked over to the attendant. "Jack, my wife needs a fishing license. Can you help her?"

"I hear she's a Cheechako. Always glad to help a Cheechako. Just fill out this piece of paper, Mrs. Sweeney, and we'll be in business."

Beth filled out the paper. She thought by now she should get used to being called a Cheechako, but somehow every time someone called her that, she felt that they were teasing her. When it was finished, she handed it Jack. "Here, Sourdough, it's all filled out."

Jack doubled up laughing at her remark. "I take it that you have been called Cheechako before. It's all in fun, Mrs. Sweeny."

"I know. You sourdoughs have different ways than what I'm used to. How much do I owe you? Give the bill to that good looking man standing beside me."

"That will be $100."

"You're kidding?"

"No, I'm afraid I'm not kidding. That's the price for outsiders."

"But I'm not an outsider. I'm married to an Alaskan and I have an Alaskan driver's license. Doesn't that make me an Alaskan?"

"I'm afraid not. Next year you will get the Alaskan resident rate of $15. But for now you have to pay the outsider's rate. It takes one year before you are actually an Alaskan resident. That's the rules."

"Really? I'm sorry," Beth said, "but I thought you were teasing when you said $100. I hope that's for the whole year."

"It is," answered Jack. "I would like to have said it was for one day, but I thought I'd already given you enough teasing for one day."

"I'll agree with that."

The two left and headed on home. It was getting late and was very dark out. In fact it had been dark for sometime. It was dark before they even went to Candice and Lonnie's house.

On the way home, Beth looked out the window. "Oh, Josh, stop! Look at the sky. What's going on? I've never seen anything like this before. Is this normal or something like outer space stuff?"

Josh grinned to himself and stopped the car. They both stepped out into the cold night air. The sky was full of different colors moving all around. The pinks, blues, whites, and greens were blended together and moved about making a wonderful display in the sky. Beth was fascinated. "It's called the aurora borealis or the northern lights. I'm always fascinating every time I see the lights. You can see it almost every night or early mornings during the wintertime. Sometimes it's more colorful than other times. We can see it from our bay window at home if you want to get back in the car."

"Do we have to leave just yet? I can't get over how beautiful the sky looks. Makes you think there has to be a God to make the sky look like this."

"You don't know if there is a God or not?"

"I just never thought too much about it. But this scene makes one think about Him, doesn't it?"

"Did you ever go to church, Beth?"

"Sure, we went to church for weddings and other special events. But we didn't go to church on Sundays."

"My folks never missed a Sunday unless they were ill. I went occasionally. Maybe we ought to find a church sometime and go. It might be good for us."

"I'm game to try anything," answered Beth.

"I'd like to take you to church one of these times. Let's plan on it. I'm just surprised you haven't been to church on Sunday. I believe that you would enjoy attending a church service," Josh said slowly.

"Like I said, I'm game to try."

Changing the subject, Josh asked, "Beth, this Saturday is the Yukon Quest. Would you like to go and see what goes on and watch the race at the beginning?"

"Sounds interesting. If we're going to be outside, I'm going to put on my warmest clothes." Beth never heard of a Yukon Quest but she would be game and would attend the event if that's what Josh wanted.

Saturday came and Josh and Beth headed to Fairbanks to see the Yukon Quest.

"Just what's a Yukon Quest?" Beth asked.

"It's a dog sled race from Fairbanks to White Horse. The mushers have dog teams that pull sleds about 1,000 miles to see which team makes it to the destination first. Next year it will be from White Horse to Fairbanks."

"It sounds interesting." Beth didn't mention that she thought that was a mean way to treat dogs making them race for miles on end in 40 degrees below weather. But this was Alaska and they had different ways she was finding out.

After they parked in Fairbanks, they made their way through

the crowd. Beth looked at the dogs all lined up. They looked so anxious to start. They were jumping around the best they could in their harnesses anticipating the starting of the race. She was surprised. If those stupid dogs were that excited about beginning the race, it must not be too hard on them. In a few seconds, it would be time for the mushers to start the race. Someone gave the signal and they were off. The excited dogs took off as if their lives depended on it.

"Those dogs act like they like this," she told Josh.

"Oh, they do. They can hardly wait to get started. They practice all year long on running with sleds. When there isn't any snow, they use sleds that slide on grass. The dogs love what they are doing."

"I'm glad you brought me. I never heard about the Yukon Quest. Do you have a special team you root for?"

"Not this year. One year I had a friend in the race and he did okay. At least he didn't come in last. But I don't know any of the mushers in today's race. It's just interesting to watch the race begin. When you think of that long drive in the cold weather, you wonder how the mushers even survive, but they come back the next year for another run. I'll confess it isn't something that I want to do."

As they drove back home, Beth wondered how many more adventures she was going to have before they stopped surprising her. She did enjoy watching the dogs get so excited about the race. It would be fun to watch the end of the race and see the reaction of the dogs when they pulled over the finish line. It would probably be more interesting watching the winning musher reach the goal line. Maybe next year when the race ends in Fairbanks, they could come back and watch the finish of the race.

Chapter 8

Bruce the Moose

osh and Beth planned to have a quiet day around the house the next day. Josh decided he would take Beth for a very short walk. They bundled up so much that Beth could hardly walk. She wasn't cold except that her eyeballs felt as though they were freezing. It was rather fun to be out in the cold air when she was dressed appropriately. The snow and ice fog made the surrounding trees a fantastic scene. When they returned they enjoyed a cup of hot chocolate, fixed a few things around the house and hung up a few pictures. It was going to be a lazy day, all in all.

When Josh went back to work, Candice came over that very day and the two ladies redecorated the house turning it from a bachelor pad to a very feminine looking home. Pretty drapes dressed the windows, throw rugs helped brighten the dull carpet, and a few knick-knacks here and there helped brighten up the place. Candice had suggested buying an attractive mirror that the two found while shopping. They located a great place for the large mirror. It would reflect the outside trees and scenic view.

The pictures they had purchased in town really turned out to be the right colors to complement the rest of the decorations. It took some doing on Candice's part to get Beth to buy the picture of the moose, but Beth finally agreed. "All Alaskans have moose pictures in their homes," she teased.

When the two finished their decorating, both women were pleased. But, Beth wasn't through yet. Another trip to town and she would get the rest of the things on her list. She didn't want to change things too fast and scare her husband out of his wits. One thing she wouldn't do and that was to decorate the garage. That was Josh's territory and she would leave it alone. It would be fun to put pink curtains in there to tease him, though. She'd have to think about that a bit more.

That evening after dinner, Beth was thinking about her improvements while she was washing dishes at the sink. She forgot about the pan on the stove with the grease in it and the smoked started pouring into the room. Quickly she removed the pan and opened the kitchen window to let the smoke escape.

Beth turned around to clean off the table and headed back to the sink again to rinse the dishcloth. She slowly backed up to the wall and stood frozen in place letting out a scream at the thing that stuck its head in her kitchen window. "Josh! Help! Come in here quick. Josh! Help!" she screamed.

Josh hurried into the kitchen and laughed as he looked at his pale and frightened wife. A moose had stuck its head right through the kitchen window over the sink and was looking all around the kitchen.

"That's only Bruce, my favorite moose, she won't hurt you." He walked over and hugged Beth. "She can't get through that small window, Beth. She's just curious about us and our house."

"So that's what a moose looks like. I've never seen anything so ugly in my life. Look, he's staring at me. I only opened the window to get a little fresh air and let the smoke out. When I turned back around he had stuck his head in the window and stared at me. He has such a huge head and a face only a mother could love. How do you get him to go away?" Beth said with tears in her eyes and a frightful look on her face.

Josh walked over to the refrigerator and took out some celery. "Here you go, Bruce, now eat your celery and be on your way." Bruce obeyed.

"Actually, Bruce is a female since there are no antlers. I should call her Brucilla, or some female name I guess," Josh laughed again trying to get his wife to lighten up a little after her fright.

"You can call her whatever you want as far as I'm concerned. So now I've seen a moose and know what one looks like in real life instead of a picture. I just didn't expect to see one up quite so close. They are ugly creatures. Its head is so big."

"You'll change your mind about the moose after you're up here for a while. The babies are so cute you want to pet them, but I wouldn't. Mamma sure wouldn't like it. And as I said, they are fascinating creatures and you'll soon get used to them. About April you'll see a cute baby moose."

"The calves would only be miniature moose, how would that be any improvement over the mama moose? I don't think I'd ever get used to having a moose stick his head through my kitchen window," she said emphatically. Beth thought she didn't even want to get used to them. Ugly wasn't a word strong enough for the creature. She hoped that would be the only moose she'd see for a very long time.

It was March now and Beth thought spring would be on its way, but it wasn't. Josh was at work and she hadn't made any effort to find a job. She was still getting used to this backward country. A knock on the door interrupted her thoughts.

"Candice, it's so nice to see you. Come in!"

"Since it's warmer out, I thought you might like to dress warmly and take a little walk with me. We still have two months before spring.

"Two months before spring? Doesn't spring come in March?"

"Not in Fairbanks, Alaska, it doesn't. It's usually around May. Get some warm clothes and let's go walking."

The two stepped out in the cool weather. It was a whole 10 degrees. But it didn't feel all that cold. It was rather nice out. At least her eyes weren't freezing. Down home she would be freezing at 10 degrees. Alaska was a strange country with strange weather. As they walked along, Beth told Candice about the moose and her kitchen window and how frightened she was.

"They are curious creatures. You should see our resident moose. We have that big bay window you saw when you came over for dinner. Well, Mr. Ed, that's what we call him, will stop by the bay window ever so often and start looking in at us while we are looking back at him. He even seems to be watching the television with us. He'll stay there around 15 minutes before he wonders off. I would love to know what he is thinking about us. He's sure is a cute animal—a good looking moose."

"Cute, you've got to be kidding. They are the ugliest creatures I've ever seen. How could you say your Mr. Ed is cute?"

"I'm going to ask you again after you've been here a year to see if you've changed your mind about Bruce. She's really a handsome moose."

Beth shook her head. "Well, I don't care if I don't ever see another moose again in my life. At least not one sticking its head in my kitchen window! Candice, I thought I was going to faint."

"If you really don't want to see another moose, you better not look over to your right, as there is one just standing by the trees staring at you," remarked Candice casually watching her friend's reaction.

"Oh, there is a moose over there. I suppose you're right and I'll get used to them sooner or later. I have a feeling it will be later," she said as she joined Candice laughing.

The long walk they took was interesting to the new Alaskan. There were scenes she would never have seen at home. Candice pointed out the blueberry patches and the low bush and high bush berry patches.

"What do you do with the berries?" Beth asked.

"Blueberries and low-bush cranberries make the best muffins, pancakes, or waffles besides wonderful jelly. Or you can make juice out of them for a tasty punch. You'll love blueberry muffins, I guarantee."

"I wouldn't begin to know how to make jelly or jam either."

"Tell you what, we'll go blueberry picking together and then I'll come over and we'll make a batch of jelly together. Or, you could ask your husband to help. He makes some very good jelly and his blueberry muffins are out of this world. You mean he hasn't made you any blueberry muffins yet?"

"No, but you can bet I'm going to ask for some tonight. I think he's trying to take this Alaskan thing slow with me. He's bound and determined to make an Alaskan out of me. What was it he called me the other day? A chec ... I can never remember that name he and Lonnie called me."

"It's called a Cheechako. It means you're new to Alaska. But you will get used to Alaskan ways. Just give yourself time and don't let Josh or Lonnie give you a bad time. How do you like

Alaska so far, Beth? Truthfully, are you happy?" questioned the friend.

"Oh, yes, Candice. I'm very happy. Josh is so good to me and we have so much fun together. It's just that everything takes a little getting used to. Alaskan ways are so different than anything I ever experienced before. I didn't think I'd ever get over that moose sticking his head in my kitchen window, but now that I think about it, it was rather funny. Then there's the cold weather that goes right through you unless you are dressed for it. But now that I know how to dress Alaskan style, I don't mind the cold weather. I'm learning a few things, but I have an idea I have a lot more things to learn and a few more shocking experiences coming."

The two headed back to Beth's house and warmed up with a cup of hot chocolate and some cookies. Beth sure enjoyed Candice and thought about what she said about the blueberries. She had never heard about low bush and high bush cranberries. It was just cranberries in the lower 48. She was anxious to make some jelly with Candice.

That evening when Josh came home from work, Beth asked him about his blueberry muffins. "I want to know how come you haven't made them for me. They sound absolutely delicious. Candice is going to teach me how to make jelly this summer."

"You want blueberry muffins for dinner tonight, you got them. You cook the rest of the dinner and I'll make the muffins."

Beth watched as Josh mixed up the muffins and added the blueberries. They looked different than any blueberries she had ever seen. They were puny little things and they looked anything but tasty. She hoped that she didn't make a mistake asking for blueberry muffins, but Candice said they were good. Well, she'd wait and see.

After sitting down at the table, the first thing Beth did was picked up a muffin and smelled it. Oh, it did smell good. Then she tasted it. It was wonderful. What a marvelous taste. She had tasted blueberry muffins before, but they didn't taste anything like this.

"These are great, Josh, ever bit as good as Candice said they would be, but how come the berries are so small?"

"They are wild Alaskan blueberries. They aren't commercial. They do have their own distinct taste," answered the muffin cook.

The two enjoyed their dinner and then Josh turned serious and looked at his wife. "Beth, we need to attend a funeral tomorrow. Jim Clawson's mother passed away. Jim has been a friend of mine for years and I feel we should attend. It's at noon. Are you up to going to a funeral?"

"Of course I'll go. But how do they bury people when the ground is so frozen. And it's piled sky high with snow. Do they have some special machinery that digs holes in that hard surface?"

"Actually, they don't bury them now. They wait until the spring thaw and then they bury the dead. Sometimes they have quite a few bodies waiting to be buried by the time the spring thaw comes."

"Are you telling me that the dead people lay there all winter long? That's awful to think about. Don't do that to me! Just cremate me and get it over with. I can't stand the idea of laying on a cold slab for months waiting for spring thaw. Ugh!"

"You wouldn't know anything about it, Beth. You would be dead."

"It's just the idea of the whole thing."

Mr. and Mrs. Sweeny went to the funeral the next day. It was a closed casket and Beth was relieved. Would she ever get used to Alaskan ways?

Chapter 9

Breakup Boots

Finally, the month of May came. Beth glanced out the window at the sun and the melting snow. She was so excited that nice weather was finally here. It was Saturday and Josh suggested they go to Fairbanks and have lunch and do some shopping. The wife was all for that.

"You need to wear these breakup boots, Darling." He handed her some big ugly boots.

"Never! Those are so ugly. I'll just wear my regular shoes, thank you. Besides it's nice outside. We don't have to dress up so much now that it's so much warmer." She didn't want to wear the ugly boots. Where did they get such a silly name as breakup boots? That name didn't make much sense to her.

Josh shook his head. It appeared that his wife would learn everything the hard way. He stuck a pair of wool socks in his pocket before going to the garage. They were soon off to Fairbanks.

"Oh, look, Josh! There's a cute little moose. Isn't he darling? A baby moose! I wish I'd brought my camera. They are darling, aren't they?"

Josh only smiled. It sure didn't take Beth long to get interested in the moose in Alaska in spite of all her resolves.

As they drove up to the parking spot, Beth looked out the window at a man passing by. "Look, Josh, at that man. He has a suit on and fancy overcoat and look at those ugly boots he's wearing. Someone ought to teach that man how to dress," Beth said as she laughed.

Josh didn't make a return comment. After he parked the car, he stepped out and walked around to Beth's car door and opened it for her. Without even looking down Beth stepped out of the car and onto what she thought would be the pavement.

"Oh, oh, there's water here. It's at least six inches deep. Oh, my feet are freezing. Oh, it's so cold," she moaned.

Josh picked up his wife and sat her back on the car seat and took off her shoes and socks. He rubbed her feet and put the extra pair of socks he brought on her feet. The wool socks quickly warmed her cold feet.

"Oh, that feels so much better, but how am I going to get into the store without any shoes?" she asked.

Josh reached in and lifted his wife out of the car and carried her toward the store.

On the way to the store Beth told him she was embarrassed that he was carrying her with everyone watching.

"Do you want me to put you down?"

"No! Are you going to buy me a pair of break-up boots?" she asked sheepishly.

"Since you asked nicely, I will. Actually, that's what we are going to do right now. J.C. Penny usually has a good supply of break-up boots this time of year. We'll try to find a really attractive pair for you."

"You know good and well that there's no such thing as an attractive pair of break-up boots. Just get me a pair and I'll wear them. You could have warned me."

"Didn't I suggest ..."

"Yeah, I guess you did. Now I know why they are called break-up boots. It's because the snow melts and breaks up. Makes sense, I guess. I thought it was just a silly name for boots."

When they stepped inside the door, Josh let Beth down. She looked around for the shoe department, but Josh took her hand and led her right to it. In minutes she was donned with break-up boots. She was almost proud of them after her experience. The wife thought that maybe she should listen to her husband a little closer if she didn't want anymore terrible experiences. She thought her feet were completely frozen after she stepped into the melting snow.

Beth saw several things she needed for the house. By the time the shopping spree was over, it was lunchtime and the two chose a French restaurant for lunch. As they entered the restaurant, they found Candice and Lonnie waiting for a table.

"Hey, you two, why don't you join us," suggested Lonnie.

"Good idea," Beth said. And the four friends had a good time of fellowship while they ate their lunch.

Candice looked at Beth. "Oh, I'm glad you have break-up boots. I was going to suggest that we'd better get them before break-up time came and then I forgot. Nice to see you are all set for this time of year."

Josh opened his mouth, but Beth warned, "One word out of you and you've had it, Mr. Sweeny."

Josh laughed so hard he almost fell off the chair. Lonnie looked at him and knew exactly what probably happened and join in the laughter.

"Don't mind them, Beth. By next year you'll know all these little things that you need to do and have in Alaska," remarked Candice. "When the weather is warmer, we want to take you to Alaska Land. It's an interesting place. And then there's the boat that goes down the Chena River and stops at a village where they work with animal skins and other things. They also stop at a dog musher's place. We'll have a good time this summer."

"Are you planning on going outside this winter," asked Lonnie.

"Going outside where? What do you mean going outside?"

"Going outside, Beth, means going down to the lower forty-eight or someplace other than Alaska. It's just an Alaskan expression," explained her husband.

"Sometimes I don't think you Alaskans always speak the King's English. Ice fog, break-up time and break-up boots, dog mushers, going outside, lower forty-eight, and Cheechako. I never heard these expressions before. Down in the 'lower forty-eight' we have dogs and cats for pets. Up here you have Mr. Ed and Bruce. It's going to take some doing to make me a … what was that name for a real Alaskan?" Beth asked.

"When they start calling you a sourdough you'll know you've been promoted to a real Alaskan."

"Are you sure it's a promotion?"

"Yes," echoed the three teasing companions.

On the way home, Beth paid special attention to the scenery. One thing about this country, it didn't lack for trees. Trees were everywhere. That was one thing that she hadn't expected. But one of the reasons she paid so much attention was that she wanted to drive to Fairbanks next week and do some shopping while Josh was at work. There were a few twists and turns to the road and she didn't want to get lost. Most of the trees were Alders and not yet showing any leaves. There were lots of green spruce trees interspersed amongst the Alders and a few other types of trees here and there. It all was so picturesque and beautiful.

Chapter 10

A New Friend

After breakfast when Josh left for work, Beth dressed in her warm clothes and made ready for a trip to Fairbanks. She needed to wait at least until 9:30 so that by the time she reached Fairbanks the stores would be open. Josh told her to be sure to watch out for the moose on the road. "And, take your cell phone with you in case you get lost," he said with a silly grin.

"I think I can find my way home. I've been riding with you to town several times. I watched all the twists and turns you've made. I promise not to get lost," she said as she kissed him goodbye.

Shopping was a lot of fun for the new wife. She wanted some things to make the master bedroom a little more attractive as well as the guest bedroom. There wasn't any furniture in the third bedroom so she wouldn't worry about that. She certainly wasn't going to worry about the attic where Josh was going to put his dozen kids.

Leisurely she shopped finding no reason to hurry. At noon she found a restaurant that looked interesting and walked in. Finding only one table empty, she sat down. After giving her order to the waitress, Beth looked around the restaurant. She loved how so many places in Alaska were attractively decorated with pictures of Eskimos and other Alaskan sites. As she studied them, a young woman approached her table.

"How about sharing your table with me, Mrs. Sweeny?" the woman asked.

Beth looked up and stared. She didn't ever remember seeing this woman before, but she wouldn't be impolite. Most of the Alaskans were really friendly. "Sure just sit down. But, I'm curious how you know my name?"

"You and Josh came to my mother-in-law's funeral. I had heard that Josh had married and took a special effort to find you in the crowd. You certainly did the impossible," the woman said.

"What do you mean I did the impossible?"

"You got that old bachelor to marry you. I would have sworn that Joshua Sweeny would never marry. He seemed to be a very happy bachelor, but from what I've heard, he's an even happier husband. Oh, by the way, my name is Vonnie Clawson and I'm really glad to meet you. I gave my order to the waitress before I sat down and it looks like our lunch is coming now."

After the waitress left, Vonnie asked her new acquaintance. "Do you mind if I pray over our meal before we eat?"

What could Beth say? This was a friend of Josh's and she didn't want to say or do the wrong thing. "Go right ahead and pray, please."

Vonnie prayed a short prayer and then began to eat. "I hear you are a city girl from the lower forty-eight. How are you enjoying life in Alaska?"

"I'm really enjoying it, but it does take a little getting used to and I don't think you Alaskans realize what a different language you speak. But I'm learning."

"Have you seen the aurora borealis yet?"

"Oh, yes, I think it was the second day I was here. I've never seen anything like it. I told my husband, it sure would make one think that there has to be a God to paint a picture like that," Beth said with enthusiasm.

"Well, there's definitely a God and He's a caring God and it's good that He made this earth with all the beautiful things such as the aurora borealis. The beautiful trees, the hills and rock formations, how could there not be a God?"

"I think you're right. I just never thought too much about it. But when I saw the aurora borealis, it seemed that it had to come from a special Being."

"Do you and Josh ever go to church, Beth?"

"We haven't, but we have talked about it from time to time. It's hard to know what church to go to. There are so many different beliefs around that I get a little mixed up thinking about it."

"Why don't you and Josh come over to our place this Sunday and come to church with us and we'll take you out to dinner afterwards at our favorite restaurant? Do you think Josh would agree? Actually, he's been to our church several times and on special occasions. He always says he feels like a fifth wheel because he didn't have a partner. Now he has one and he might be more comfortable."

"Give me you phone number, Vonnie, and I'll ask Josh if he will come Sunday and then I'll call you with the answer. I think I would like to go. It was never a priority with my parents, but I'm interested in going to church at least one time," exclaimed Beth. "After that I can decide if I want to go back again or not."

"Josh has our phone number, but I'll give it to you anyway." Vonnie wrote down the number on a piece of paper and handed it to Beth. They had finished eating and were ready to leave. The two walked toward the door. As Vonnie stepped out of the restaurant door, she added, "See you Sunday, Beth. Goodbye."

Beth didn't quite know what to think. Vonnie was a very nice person even though she was religious. She could never remember anyone praying over a meal and thanking God for the food, but she thought it was rather nice. Beth was hoping that Josh would agree to go to church next Sunday. For some reason, she really wanted to go. It was strange, as she never had any interest before in attending church. Maybe it's just an Alaskan thing, she thought as she anticipated the conversation she would have with her husband that evening.

Beth finished all her shopping. It was almost two o'clock by the time she headed down the road toward home in the small pickup. Josh always took the automobile but he had the pickup for hauling things to the dump and carrying home big items from the store. It appeared a pickup was a necessary thing in Alaska.

As she drove along, her mind was on what Vonnie had said. She couldn't shake the feeling that Vonnie had something she didn't have. Her thoughts were interrupted as she glanced down the road and saw a moose right in the middle of the road. Beth slowed the pickup down to see what the moose would do. It wandered to the side of the road. She let out her breath and drove on, but just as she was about to drive past where the moose left the road, it turned around and ran right back onto the road and into her pickup.

Beth slammed on the breaks. The moose, a little dazed, walked off into the woods. The shocked woman noticed a car pulling up beside her pickup. It was a police car. Was there some fine for hitting a moose? But she didn't hit it; the moose hit her.

"Are you okay, Ma'am?" the officer asked.

"I don't know, a little shook up. What does my pickup look like on that side where the moose hit it?"

"Looks a little beat up. Do you always go around running over moose, Mrs. Sweeny?" the officer asked in a teasing manner.

"If you were watching you know good and well that that moose hit me, I didn't hit him."

"He's a she."

"I don't care, he or she, I didn't hit that silly moose." Beth knew the officer was only teasing, but she was still shook up from the whole experience.

"I saw the whole thing and I know what the moose did, but I have to tease the new Cheechakoes in our area, don't I?"

"How do you now that I'm a Cheechako?"

"Because you are Mrs. Joshua Sweeny, that's how I know. You have captured the one man that couldn't be caught. He had a lot of ladies chasing him through the years he lived up here. He didn't look twice at them. How did you ever get him to marry you? It puzzles all his friends."

"We had a lot of help from both our parents. I don't think we had a choice," laughed Beth. "So, I assume you know Josh."

"Everyone knows Josh. He's been here quite a while. You have a good man there, Mrs. Sweeny."

"You could call me Beth."

"If you'll call me Joe, it's a deal. I imagine you want to wait until Josh sees this pickup and let's you know where you can get it fixed. It's just the passenger's door that is messed up. Hopefully it won't cost too much after your insurance pays their part. I'll say goodbye and be on my way. It was nice meeting you, Beth."

"It was nice meeting you, Joe. Thanks for calming me down.

Now I just have to face that husband of mine. You'll tell him the moose hit me won't you?"

"I could be bribed to do that," the officer said and grinned as he walked back to his police car.

So many cars had passed them as the policeman was talking to her. She wondered how many of them knew that it was Josh's pickup that the moose run into. Beth was hoping that no one knew. Even though it wasn't her fault, she didn't want people to know what happened. For some reason she felt embarrassed.

Chapter 11

An Invitation to Church

Beth looked out the window and saw Josh drive in the driveway. He deliberately walked over to the passenger side of the pickup and looked it over. He was even smiling over the damage. How did he know anything had happened to his pickup? It wasn't parked so he could see the damage from his car when he drove in the driveway. Beth wondered who had blabbed the news!

Josh came into the house. "I heard you were running over moose today since you didn't have anything else to do."

"And just where did you hear that? From Joe, I presume?"

"Yes, I heard it from Joe, Jim, and a half dozen other people. Joe said you ran right into that moose and didn't even give the poor thing a chance to get out of the way."

Beth put her hands on her hips and glared at her husband saying nothing. Josh broke down and laughed so hard she thought he was having a heart attack.

"Did Joe tell you what happened?"

"Yeah, he did. Just think of it this way, Beth. They say that when people have been in Alaska long enough, they will hit a moose sooner or later. You just got yours sooner and now you don't have to worry about it later."

"Funny."

"I'll take the pickup to work tomorrow and check on the repairs on my lunch hour. I may call you to come pick me up after work, okay?"

"Be sure to warn the moose!"

"I'll put a sign out on the road so the moose will know you're coming," Josh said in a very serious voice.

Beth turned towards the kitchen. It was time to start dinner and forget about that miserable moose. Hopefully, that's the last time that something like that would happen to her.

While they were eating supper, Beth remembered Vonnie's conversation. "Josh, we were invited to church this Sunday and out to lunch after church. Are you interested?"

"You must have met Vonnie. What did you tell her?"

"How did you know it was Vonnie? There are other people in the church that could have invited us. Anyway, I told her I'd talk with you. I'd really like to go. She's a neat gal. I did enjoy having lunch with her."

"Yeah, that's what Jim said. I told him we would go. I'm glad you want to go or I'd be in trouble about now. I'm glad you like Vonnie. She and Jim have been my friends since I first came up here. I used to go to church with them all the time and then I got busy building my home and just got out of the habit of going."

"So you know what her church is like, then. I shouldn't be so surprised that you used to go to church."

"Why do you say that?"

"You don't swear; that's one of the first things I noticed."

"You don't swear either and you're not a church attendee. What other reason do you have to think I was brought up in church?"

"You've never taken me to a bar and I don't see even a beer

in your refrigerator. You've never ordered any liquor when we've gone out to dinner."

"Did you want to order some?"

"Not really. I never liked the taste of liquor. I only ordered a drink to be polite when my friends did," Beth admitted.

"Beth, I think you'll like the church. The people are very friendly and the services are good. So, we'll plan on going Sunday."

"Okay. Now I have to figure out what to wear. Maybe I should buy a new outfit. What do you think?"

"Honey, if you want a new outfit, go get it. But some ladies wear slack outfits, some casual clothes and some really dress up. There's no real dress code, except I wouldn't want you to wear beach clothes to church," Josh said as he smiled that teasing smile he did so often.

"So I can just wear what I wore out to dinner, then?"

"That's right. Now let me help you with the dishes since you shopped all day and ran over a moose. You're probably pretty tired." Josh ducked at she took a swing at him. He shouldn't bring up the moose, but it was so hard not to.

Beth decided to ignore his remark about the moose. The more fuss she made the more he was going to tease her. Candice was right. Just ignore him.

"Hey, Honey, I have a book for you to read. It's required reading for all Alaskan residents."

"Okay, I'll bite. What's the name of the book?" He was pulling her leg again.

"No, I'm serious. I think you would like this book. It's about a girl that comes up to Alaska to be a schoolteacher a good many years ago. It's a true story. It's called *Tisha*. The Eskimo children couldn't pronounce teacher so that's what they came up with.

There are a few bad words in it that could have been left out, but she put in everything that happened including the cuss words. I'll get it for you. Once you read it you'll think you have life easy." Josh walked into the library and brought the book and Beth set it aside to read at a later time.

After Josh went to work the next day and when all her housework was finished, Beth sat down and picked up the book. She started reading. She sure didn't want to go through some of the experiences this gal went through. It must have been rough in Alaska in the early days. She couldn't imagine riding a horse that long ways to a town called Chicken. Neither could she imagine going out in the freezing weather and having to use the outhouse. Ugh! She was almost through the book when she heard a knock on the door.

"Come in, Candice. It's good to see you. What's going on in your life?"

"Not much. I hear you are going to church Sunday with Vonnie and Jim. I think you'll enjoy it. They also called us and asked us to come along and go out to dinner as well. I'm looking forward to it. Lonnie and I used to go all the time and we just got busy and once you don't go, it's hard to get started back."

"That's exactly what Josh said. I guess I'm the only person whose never really attended church except for wedding and funerals and special occasions. I guess I better shape up," Beth remarked.

"Don't worry about it, Beth, you'll like it fine."

"My parents never thought it necessary to go to church. Just be a good citizen and you'll be all right is what they believed. I just hope I'm not getting into something I shouldn't. But talking with Vonnie, it seemed the right thing to do. I suppose it won't hurt me to go to church once in my life time."

"I'd be willing to bet you want to go back."

"You think so, huh?"

"I'll bet you dinner a week from this coming Sunday after church that you'll want to go again," laughed Candice. "Is it a bet?"

"It's a bet. McDonalds is open on Sunday isn't it?"

"You lose the bet and you're not going to get by with McDonalds," stated Candice emphatically.

Chapter 12

Trout Fishing

When Candice visited the next day, the two had a cup of coffee together and Beth asked about berry picking. "You mentioned blue berries and cranberries or something. When do we go berry picking?"

"I'm sorry but the blueberries don't come on until August. The low bush and high bush cranberries will be ready a little later. We just have to wait. The summer will be full of lots of other things to do. We go down to the Kenai Peninsula to dip net salmon and fish for halibut in July."

"Do we get a motel room or something or does Josh have friends down there?"

"Hasn't Josh shown you his motor home yet? It's a big one and he takes that down to the peninsula and parks it at the house of a friend of his where he can hook it up to electricity. We usually all go together and have a great time."

"I can hardly wait. What do we do in May and June if there's no berry picking?"

"I'll take you trout fishing. Want to go tomorrow?"

"Why not?"

After the two had coffee and cookies, Candice decided it was time to head for home. "Be ready about nine in the morning and we'll head for the river. Why don't we get together at my place and have a fish fry afterwards?"

"You seem pretty sure you're going to catch some fish. I hate to tell you this but I've never been fishing in my life. I don't know anything about it. You sure you want to take on a beginner."

"You'll probably out fish me. Just be ready to go. I'll bring the fishing poles and the bait and the fish box. You bring a snack in case we get hungry, agreed?"

After Candice left, Beth wondered what she was getting into, but then every new adventure was fun, except maybe the two moose meetings. Beth thought about what Candice first said about hearing she was going to church. Everyone knew that she hit a moose or actually the moose hit her. Everyone knew that Josh got married and that he married a newcomer. There sure was no keeping a secret in this place. Too many people knew Joshua Sweeny.

That evening, Beth told Josh of their plans to go fishing. "I'm envious of Candice," he said. "I wanted to teach you to fish, but you'll have a good time. What are you going to do with all the fish you bring back?"

"What makes you think we're going to catch any fish?"

"You will."

"To answer your question, we're invited over to Candice and Lonnie's for a fish fry, what ever that is. I hope I don't fall in the river or do some dumb thing while I'm fishing. You know I've never been before."

"You'll be just fine. You'll have the time of your life. Go and have fun and I'll look forward to eating fish tomorrow night. Wait just a minute and let me get you some mosquito repellent.

It's about time for those miserable insects to start attacking us and they can bite."

Josh left the room and came back shortly with a bottle of liquid. "Just spread this all over everywhere that flesh is showing. Then the mosquitoes won't bite you."

Beth took a smell. "Oh, that smells awful, I think I'll pass. I've never been bothered by mosquitoes."

"Beth, take it with you in case you change your mind," suggested her husband.

Beth frowned, but decided she would do as he asked and she put the bottle in her purse. It would have to be pretty bad mosquitoes before she put any of that stuff on her. Sometimes Josh was like an old grandmother.

"You and Candice seem so sure we are going to catch some fish. What if we don't, then what will we have for dinner?"

"You'll catch fish, guaranteed!" smiled the husband.

Nine o'clock the next morning, Beth looked out her window to see Candice drive up in her pickup. The new fisher woman was out the door and down the steps in seconds to start this new adventure. Candice greeted her and the two were off for a drive to the river that looked very interesting.

Upon arriving at the river bank, Beth started to get her pole out of the back of the pickup when a bunch of mosquitoes came after her, swirling around her head. "Oh, that one bit me." She ran for the pickup and generously spread the mosquito repellent all over her bare places.

"I thought you already had mosquito repellent on," Candice said. "Didn't that Josh tell you about putting on insect repellent? He ought to be kicked if he didn't. The mosquitoes here will drive you crazy if you don't use repellent."

"Oh, he did. I just didn't think I'd need it. But I changed my mind. This is much better. Now where's my pole?"

Candice picked up Beth's fishing pole, put some salmon eggs on the hook and threw the line into the river for her. "That's how you do it, Beth. The next time you have to do it yourself. Just hold the pole until you feel something tugging on it."

"You mean like this." Beth's line was already pulling and moving around. "What do I do now?"

"Start reeling."

"Start what?"

"Turn the little handle there forward. That's right. You're doing great. Keep reeling. You almost have the fish on the land. There you got it."

"What do I do now?"

"You take the fish off the hook," exclaimed the fishing teacher.

Beth looked at the squirming fish. "It won't hold still."

Candice reeled in her pole and put it down. "I only do this once for you, partner, and you have to do it next time, okay?" Candice held the fish in one hand and reached for the end of the hook with her other hand and carefully removed the hook from the fish's mouth. "This is a nice size fish for a trout. That was fast work. Are you ready to try for another one?"

"I guess. First I put these eggs on the hook. Now I throw it out … oops. It's up in the tree. What do I do now?"

"Guess!"

"I either yank it down or climb up after it," Beth answered.

"You got that right."

Beth yanked on the pole real hard and the line came flying out of the tree and almost hit Candice in the head with the hook and sinkers. With all the effort pulling on the line, Beth lost her balance and landed right in the middle of a mud puddle. Standing up, she managed to apologize to her fishing partner. She ignored the mud-splattered clothing she was now wearing.

"Oh, I'm sorry I almost hit you. I'll try to do better this time." Beth picked up the pole and examined it. "That tree ate all my salmon eggs. I am going to learn how to do this right, Candice. I really am!" The new fisher woman put more eggs on the hook.

"Wait before you throw it back out," Candice instructed her beginner trainee. "Now hold the pole up back over your shoulder and when you throw it out, throw it straight out in front of you."

Beth followed her instructions and smiled. It didn't go too far, but it went into the water. "Do I need to throw the line out further than this or will this do? "

"Leave it there for a while and see if you get any bites and if not, you can throw it out further."

About that time, Beth had another bite and this time she knew exactly what to do with the fish she had caught. She began reeling and the trout came right up on the bank. She picked it up and proceeded to get the hook out of the trout's mouth as she had seen Candice do. "Ouch, that hook is sharp. I'm bleeding."

"You'll do better next time, Cheechako," laughed Candice. "There's a band-aid in the tackle box, help yourself. Put your fish in the fish box. You know that I haven't caught my first fish yet and you've caught two plus the tree and your finger. I'd call that beginners luck." Candice was really laughing now and Beth joined her.

"You'd probably have your box full if it wasn't for teaching me," Beth remarked. She put the bandage over her bleeding finger and proceeded to put more salmon eggs on the hook. It wasn't long before both ladies were catching fish and soon had their limit.

"Well, we have to quit now," Candice said.

"Why, it's early, only eleven o'clock. We have lots of time."

"Beth, we can only catch five trout each. No more. That's the law."

"Oh, and I was just getting the hang of it. I think I might make a fisher person yet."

"Well, you out fished me. You caught six out of the ten."

"I had a great time and a good teacher. So now we take them home and clean them, right?"

"No," Candice replied, "we're going to clean them here. Then we don't have the mess at the house. I'll get the cleaning board out and the knives and show you how it's done."

Although it was a little disgusting at first, it didn't take long before Beth was cleaning her share of the fish. She had suggested that since she caught six fish that Candice should clean six fish to make up for it. Candice just shook her head and told her fishing partner to keep cleaning.

When Josh came home, Beth was excited about telling him how the fishing trip went. "I even caught more than Candice did," she said.

"I heard you caught a tree too."

"Where did you hear that?"

"Word gets around."

The two headed for Candice and Lonnie's place. Beth was hoping she would like to eat the trout as much as she liked to catch them.

After tasting the fish, Beth thought the trout was the best tasting fish she'd ever eaten. The four laughed as she told them of her catching the tree and slipping in the mud and almost hitting Candice in the head with her hook. Beth even showed them her wound from the hook.

Lonnie couldn't resist a teasing remark. "Just have a little patience with this Cheechako, Candice, she'll learn in time. Did she put the mosquito repellent on that Josh gave her even though she didn't like the smell?"

"After the first mosquito bite with a dozen flying around her head, she ran to the car and doused herself with it," laughed Candice.

"My Cheechako learns things the hard way," replied Josh.

One of these times when those two men call her a Cheechako, she was going to think of a good retaliation reply. Right now she couldn't think of anything to say so she gave them a mean glance. It wouldn't have mattered anyway. Lonnie would have paid no attention to anything she said. He just loved to tease anyone and Josh was just like him. She had to learn not to pay any attention to either of them when it came to teasing, which was most of the time.

It had been a good day, she thought, and a fun time visiting with her friends. She had learned how to catch fish, how to cook them, and certainly had no trouble learning how to eat them. She could hardly wait to go fishing again.

Chapter 13

A New Experience

Sunday morning came and Beth dressed for church. She was a little nervous thinking about it and then she thought how foolish that was. Her friends and Josh used to go to church all the time and they were good people.

When they entered the church, some of the people came up and shook hands with her and Josh. They welcomed them into the service and told them they hoped to see them come again.

The service opened in prayer and was followed by a lively song service, which Beth really enjoyed. Beth loved to sing and she caught on quickly to the tune as she looked at the words in the songbook. The special solos were excellent. Beth had a keen ear for music and was impressed at the music presentation.

The sermon followed and she listened intently. She had decided that she was going to do this church business up right to see if it was something she wanted to do in the future. As she listened to the sermon, she could never remember hearing anything remotely resembling what the preacher was saying. She took out her pen and wrote down the scriptures that the minister quoted and determined that she was going to look them up and check on the words to make sure that was what was written in the Bible.

After the service, more people came up and welcomed them

and invited them back. The pastor shook their hands and mentioned how glad he was that they came. "Please don't stay away so long next time, Josh. We miss you."

"We'll try to do better in the future, Pastor. It was a good service and it was good to be here today," Josh said goodbye to the pastor and the two left.

Vonnie and Jim took their four friends out to their favorite restaurant. Beth really enjoyed the fellowship and the interesting conversation the six had while eating their meal. There were a few words over the bill, but Vonnie insisted that she and Jim would be paying the bill as promised and finally the two men relented and let them pay for the meals.

"Okay," Beth exclaimed, "but next Sunday we pay."

No one said a word. All of them were wondering what Beth's feelings about the church service were, but since she was coming back next Sunday, they just smiled. Candice wanted so much to remind Beth of the bet they had made earlier in the week, but she wouldn't. Things were turning out right and she wouldn't say anything.

At home, Josh asked her about the service, if she enjoyed it. "I did, Josh, very much. I wrote some scriptures down that the minister had quoted. I want to look them up and read them for myself. I know that sounds awful, but I've never heard anything that even resembled what he was talking about. Where could we buy a Bible?"

"I have one in the bedroom. Just a minute," and he headed for the bedroom.

"You have a Bible?"

"You didn't think I was a heathen, did you?"

"It doesn't mean you're a heathen if you don't have a Bible. If it does, I guess I'm a heathen."

"Here you are." He handed her the Bible and a little booklet. She put it aside. Tomorrow she would look up those scriptures. Somehow she was sure they were exactly as the minister quoted, but she still wanted to look up the scriptures and read them herself.

"Would you like to run down to the river for an hour or so and catch some more fish for tonight?"

"Yes," Beth exclaimed excitedly. "It was so much fun the other day even if I did catch the tree, cut my finger on the hook and fell into a mud puddle. What can be more fun than that?" she laughed.

Down at the river, Josh met some friends already fishing. He introduced Beth to Alex and Marian Jensen.

"I'm really glad to meet you, Beth. I heard you were quite a fisher woman, able to shake out fish hooks in tall trees and jump over fishing equipment and land in soft places on the ground," Alex remarked with a teasing grin on his face as well as in his voice. "That's pretty good for a first time fisher woman."

"Nothing is private up here in Alaska is it? You heard this from Candice?"

"No, a friend of mine was fishing down below and saw the whole thing. He laughed so much he almost fell in the river," answered Alex.

"It would have served him right if he had fallen in the water. Anyway, it's nice to meet you, I think." Beth picked up her fishing pole and put the salmon eggs on the hook and threw the line into the water. In only one minute or two, she pulled out a nice trout. To Josh's amazement, she took it off the hook and put it in the fish box and put a few more eggs on her hook. Beth never said anything to any of them. They could make fun of her first fishing trip if they wanted to, but she was hoping to out fish all of them this afternoon—at least out fish Alex.

It seemed to Beth that everything she did was spread all over town. Maybe this was what they did to all Cheechakoes. She supposed it was funny, but she wasn't about to let them know it. Oops, there's another fish. Beth pulled it in again without saying anything and put it in the fish box. No one else had caught anything as yet.

"Just what are you doing that the fish are biting your hook and not mine?" ask Alex. "You are a beginner and a Cheechako at that. You're not supposed to out fish all the rest of us."

"It's all in the wrist," Beth stated.

Josh was the next one to bring in a trout and finally Alex brought one in but not before Beth had her third one. Marian brought in the next two. When Beth had five trout, she went to the pickup and took out a soda and sat down and watched.

"Hey, partner, you're supposed to be fishing. What are you doing sitting down on the job?" Josh asked.

"I caught my five and that's all I'm allowed to catch. If I catch anymore I'd be breaking the law. So catch another three fish and then we can go home."

Josh smiled at his wife. He was glad that she had out fished them all and more than glad that she enjoyed fishing so much. He could hardly wait until he took her salmon and halibut fishing. If she liked fishing for these trout, which were a good size for trout, what would she do when she caught a big salmon? He sure enjoyed watching his wife as she experienced each new adventure in Alaska.

"We can't eat more than seven fish anyway. I vote we call it quits." Josh picked up the poles and put them in the back of the pickup. After putting fish and tackle boxes in the pickup they said goodbye to their friends and headed home.

"How many of these fish can you eat tonight," Josh asked.

"Only one is all I want. They are pretty good size," Beth answered.

"I'll prepare the other five fish for the freezer and we'll save them for another day," Josh said.

Beth cooked the trout just as she had watched Candice cook the other night. She did like to eat the trout almost as much as she liked fishing for them. After the dishes were done, the two watched television and then headed for bed.

After Josh left for work the next day, Beth picked up the little booklet that Josh gave her. She read it through. It had the same scripture verses that the minister had quoted at church. She looked up John 3:16 and read it. "For God so loved the world that He gave His only begotten Son that whosoever believeth in Him shall not perish but have everlasting life." That verse along with the others backed up everything the pastor said.

Beth bowed her head and prayed. "God, I don't know anything about religious things, but I do believe that You gave Your Son to die for me. Please forgive me for the things I've done wrong. Amen." She wondered if there was something else she was supposed to do, but if so, she'd find out in church. She would listen carefully and perhaps even take notes from the sermon to study when she returned home.

When Josh came in that evening, she told him about her prayer. "Beth, I think that's wonderful. I prayed that prayer when I was younger and have been a Christian most of my life, but sometimes I get careless. Not anymore, though. We're going to make our home a Christian home."

Beth came over and hugged her husband. He was such a good man. God had been good to her to let her marry Josh even when she didn't even recognize there was a God.

Chapter 14

The Gold Panning Experience

"I have two days off, Beth. Let's take that boat trip down the Chena and let you see some great scenery and visit an Eskimo village and a dog musher's ranch. It's nice weather now. We might even visit Alaska Land. It's rather a unique place. There's lots of history in that park."

"Candice was telling me about it. Are we going tomorrow?"

"That's the plan. Wear comfortable shoes as we may do some walking. And take a warm jacket. Sometimes on the river it gets a little cooler than on land. Oh, yes, Candice and Lonnie are coming."

"Great. They add fun to any outing. What time do we take off in the morning?"

"I thought we might eat breakfast in town and then head for the boat. I believe it leaves at ten."

The next morning they met Lonnie and Candice for breakfast and then headed for the big boat. Beth was so fascinated when they stopped at the Eskimo village. They were tanning hides that would be made into moccasins or coats. They even made thimbles out of the hide. She supposed that was for the tourists' benefit. They had several items they were making that they would eventually sell at the markets down town. Josh had informed her that the Eskimos called themselves Inupiat, which means the people. Beth found that interesting. Probably at one time they thought they were the only people on the planet. She enjoyed seeing all the things the Eskimos made.

As she surveyed the Chena River, she noticed how wide and spread out it was. It wandered all over the place. It certainly was a different type of river than she had ever seen before. The weather was so nice and the scenery great. Now she understood a little more how Josh fell in love with Alaska. There was no scenery anywhere else that even compared to the scenery found in the land of Alaska.

Candice came over and stood beside her. "Amazing country, isn't it?"

"It sure is. I can't get over this. About the time I think I've seen a lot of Alaska, I see something else interesting. This has been a great boat ride. I wouldn't mind taking the trip again. You said we're going to go through Alaska Land when we get back, is that right?"

"Yes, we should have timed it just right so we can eat there. They cook salmon, halibut, trout, and other foods. They have lots of salad and baked potatoes. They put the side dishes in caches and you walk from one cache to another to fill up your plate. It's fun. The first time we ate at Alaska Land, the governor was right there eating with us. We felt privileged to have dinner with the governor of the state of Alaska even though he didn't know we were there," Candice informed her.

"It does sound like something interesting to do."

Beth wasn't quit ready to get off the boat when the time came, but she did. It wouldn't hurt her feeling to turn around and go right back down the Chena River.

The four of them toured Alaska Land and stopped at most

of the tourist shops. They had some interesting things for sale. Beth bought a few things that fascinated her. As she looked around, she knew these shops were set up especially for tourists. Well, she was new enough to Alaska to be called a tourist.

The dinner was everything that Candice had told her it would be. She took the halibut and filled the rest of her plate with the salad and breads and potatoes. It all looked good and smelled even better. The pies were especially tasty. Although the four of them enjoyed their day, they were ready to go home. It had been a full day and then some and Beth knew that the bed would feel good tonight.

The next morning Josh had a suggestion. "Since I have one more day off, how would you like to go gold panning?"

"Doesn't that sound like fun?"

"You did remember that tomorrow was your birthday? I talked to a friend of mine who owns a gold mining operation and he said to bring you out there on your birthday and he would scoop some stuff out of the sluice box and let us pan it. That way you will be sure and get some gold."

"What time do we leave?"

"We better start at eight as it's quite a drive up there. Now I don't want you to get the wrong idea because gold panning is just plain hard work. Your arms will get tired and you'll wonder if you're ever going to get the gold out of the pan."

"It still sounds interesting to me."

The two left at eight the next morning and headed for the gold mine. Beth watched the scenery as they drove. They went past the pipeline that she had heard so much about. That was an interesting sight. Josh pointed out the good blueberry patches along the way as well as a bear or two. Did she want to pick blueberries if there was a chance of a bear showing up in the patch of berries?

"Do bears come around when you are picking blueberries?"

"If you make enough noise you'll probably never see any bears. They aren't anymore happy to see you than you are to see them. It's perfectly safe if you just use a little common sense. I've picked blueberries every year since I came up here and never ran into a bear even once."

Finally they arrived at the gold mining operation. Beth looked at all the equipment located around the area. Quite an operation, she thought. Josh ushered her over and introduced her to his friend.

"Hi, Melvin, meet my wife, Beth. She would like to do a little gold panning. As I told you it's her birthday. Where do you want us to work?"

"Stand right over there and I'll get you both a pan." Melvin scooped the pans into the sluice box and handed one to each of them. "Now you put a little water in there and shake it around like this." Melvin swished the gold pan around in a circle movement. The dirt washes out of the pan and the gold goes to the bottom. It will take you a while to do it, but in the end, you'll find some gold in the bottom of the pan."

Beth watched how Josh swished his pan around and started swishing hers the same way. This was fun she thought at first. After half an hour, she wasn't quite sure that gold panning was all that much fun. After one hour she didn't think she could shake the stupid pan one more time and Beth sat back and rested. Melvin came over and after a few swishes, showed her the gold in the bottom of the pan. Beth was shocked. She really didn't think there was anything but sand and dirt in that pan and there were the shining flakes of gold.

Melvin handed her the pan back and she felt the gold. It was amazing. Then she turned to Josh and said, "I'm through, how come you're so slow?"

"At least I can claim I did mine all by myself. I'm almost through. We should have a nice bit of gold here."

"What will we do with it now?" Beth asked.

"We'll take it to the jeweler I know in Fairbanks and have them make you a nice necklace. We should have enough gold to make necklaces for you and our mothers for Christmas. What do you think? Is that a good idea?"

"What a great idea! Do you always find gold when you go gold panning?"

"Not always, but we were sure to find it this time because it was taken out of a sluice box. All the sand and dirt came right out of the mine. Someday we'll go down to a stream and do a little gold panning there if you want to, but I can't promise you that we'll get any gold there."

"Right now I don't know if my arm will ever swish a gold pan again. That's nothing but hard work."

"You got that right!" said her husband. "But it was fun too, now admit it."

"Yes, it was. Now if I ever get over my sore arm, I'll be happier about everything. I guess people who do a lot of panning obtain the right muscles sooner or later."

Melvin gave Josh a little box to put the gold in and the two headed for Fairbanks. The gold mine was quite some miles away from Fairbanks. The two went directly to the jewelry store.

The jeweler told them it would take a week before the necklaces would be ready but they had plenty of gold to make three necklaces. "You actually have enough gold if you wanted to make a couple tie tacks for your fathers."

"Oh, yes, please make the tie tacks," Beth said.

When the week was over, Beth could hardly wait to pick them up. She headed for Fairbanks as soon as she thought the jewelry store would be open. When he handed her the necklaces and tie tacks, she was surprised. They were beautiful. And she had panned some of the gold herself! What a neat experience. She would make sure that her mother and dad knew that she was responsible for some of the gold in the necklaces and the tie tacks. Beth knew that would make the jewelry all the more special to her parents.

Chapter 15

The Bear Encounter

Beth couldn't believe how beautiful the area was as far as she could see. And the weather was so perfect she hated to stay indoors. Taking the mosquito repellent she had purchased yesterday, she sprayed the repellent everywhere there was a piece of skin showing. Then Beth stepped out of the house and went for a walk. The wildflowers were out in full bloom and covered the area. She was determined to pick a bouquet for her table. There were so many different types of wildflowers. She would have to ask Josh where she could find a book that would tell her the names of the flowers.

June had been such a fun month. She and Candice had traipsed all over the area. Beth had every intention of applying for a job, but now with the nice weather, she didn't want to miss a day exploring the area. It would be a long winter when it came so she was determined to make good use of every day of the summer. In just days they would be heading down to the Kenai Peninsula for salmon and halibut fishing. All winter Candice, Lonnie, and Josh talked about the trip and now she was excited to go.

Beth had every intention of staying outside for a long walk, but she suddenly changed her mind. Not too far away from her was a black bear looking right at her. Beth said a quick prayer for help and then remembered what Josh had said about making a lot of noise. So she began to sing and kick rocks and anything she could think of that would make noise as she gradually and slowly made her way back to the house. The bear ignored her and slowly walked off. Perhaps a better use of her time would be to plant some flowers around the house. She didn't want to encounter another bear any too soon.

That evening, she told Josh about her experience with the bear. "He didn't pay a whole lot of attention to me when I started making noise. I wanted to run for the house, but I remembered that you said not to. Prey run from bears and I sure didn't want to be his next meal."

"One thing I might tell you. If you ever go fishing and there's a bear there, let him have the fishing hole and you find another one. After all he was here first and has first rights to the fishing hole. Okay?"

"Okay, I won't argue with a bear over a fishing hole," she agreed hoping that she would never see a bear up that close again. After that experience, Beth kept an eye out for bears whenever she went walking. The summer days were passing a little too quickly to please the young woman.

It was the middle of July and tomorrow they would leave on the trip to go salmon dip netting, and salmon and halibut fishing on the Kenai Peninsula. It sounded like so much fun that she could barely wait to go. If salmon fishing was half as much fun as trout fishing, she knew she was in for a great time.

Josh took her out and showed her the motor home. It was a nice one. He explained what all they needed to pack and asked her to pack enough for several meals and when they ran out of food they would either eat out or buy some more groceries. So the potential traveler sat down and made her list of meals for a week. Although the refrigerator wasn't too big, she felt she could fit in all the items that needed refrigeration.

The phone rang and Beth picked it up. It was her mom again. Beth didn't need to call her folks, as they always beat her to the punch. The new Alaskan told her mom all about the bear, the gold panning, and the trout fishing among other things.

"Beth, you do live a busy life up there in Alaska. You sound so happy and pleased with your life. I'm glad, Darling. It isn't so bad when I can pick up the phone and talk to you now and then. We are talking about a trip up to Alaska but your dad's work seems to forbid it right now. We'll see if we can work it in at a later time."

The two talked for quite a while before saying goodbye. After she hung up, she thought how nice it would be if her mom and dad did come to visit.

Chapter 16

The Kenai Peninsula

The next morning they were all packed and ready to go when Candice and Lonnie arrived. They would leave their car parked in Josh's driveway. Lonnie moved their luggage to the motor home and shortly the four of them were driving down the road towards Fairbanks and on down the road to Anchorage and then on to the Kenai Peninsula. Beth was determined to see as much scenery as possible on the way to the peninsula.

As they drove down the highway, she noticed the tall regal mountain tips and rugged hills. It was all so beautiful that she couldn't take her eyes from the scenes. There had to be a God that made all this scenery look so enticing. And she knew there was a God the day that she gave her heart to the Lord. It was a special time when she asked God to forgive her of her sin and she accepted Him as her Savior. It gave her a whole different outlook on life.

"Enjoying the ride, Darling?" Josh asked.

"It's a gorgeous drive. I've never seen anything like this before. There are so many different scenic views all the way down to Anchorage. Alaska must be one of God's special places because He made it so beautiful. I don't think there's any other place like it in the world," answered the wife.

"That's the way I felt the first time I drove this road. It has to be the most fascinating drive in the world, at least as far as I'm concerned. We are going to pass Denali Park pretty soon. Most Americans call it Mt. McKinley, but the Eskimos and Alaskans call it Denali. One of these days, we'll take the bus ride through Denali Park. You'll see a lot of different animals. It's a big mountain, one of the biggest around."

"I'd like to do that. Alaska never fails to fascinate me. Everything is so different than LA or Ohio. There's nothing that compares to this."

"We keep telling you that Alaska is bigger and better than anywhere else in the world," Lonnie reminded her.

"I'm beginning to believe you," the new comer assented.

"Beth, you want to have some coffee, tea, or hot chocolate? We brought a thermos of each one." remarked Candice.

"Hot chocolate does sound good. I have some cookies to go along with it. How about you guys, anything sound good to you?"

"I'll have coffee," the two echoed.

"Coming right up," Candice said as she poured the coffee and then delivered it to the men. Josh pulled off to a rest stop.

"Want me to drive for a while, partner?" asked Lonnie.

"That's a good idea. I'm getting a little road weary."

They all stepped out of the motor home and stretched as they looked over the inviting scenery. "I'd sure like to scale that mountain, but I guess that will have to be another time or we'll never get to the peninsula," remarked Lonnie.

Beth was fascinated when Lonnie drove through Anchorage. Fairbanks was a small town compared to where she used to live.

Anchorage was more like a real city. All the tall buildings and stores just invited her to go shopping. She had to get Josh to bring her shopping in Anchorage or talk Candice into driving down and going shopping. She didn't know that there was a city as big as Anchorage in all of Alaska. Fairbanks was the biggest one she had seen at this point in time. All the other little towns they had driven through were hardly big enough to be called towns.

Driving down to the peninsula was another pleasant experience to the new Alaskan. More beautiful scenery and gorgeous mountains everywhere she looked along with beautiful flowers. Finally, they arrived in Soldotna and pulled into a driveway. It was very late and Josh explained that they would just park here for the night, and in the morning he would talk to his friends about where to park the motor home.

Beth had never slept in a motor home, but she had no problem going to sleep. She couldn't get over the clean fresh air that was so prevalent in Alaska that certainly wasn't in Los Angeles. Tomorrow morning they were going dip netting. Whatever that was, she had no idea. But she was tired of portraying herself as ignorant and decided to just wait and see what dip netting was all about. Josh had explained to her that she wouldn't be able to dip net herself, but she could watch and help take care of the fish.

Kirk Westland came out of his house the next morning as soon as he saw someone stirring in the motor home. He had met Lonnie and Candice before and nodded hello. He stared at the new face with a puzzled look.

Josh spoke up quickly. "Kirk, I want you to meet my wife, Beth."

Kirk stared at her for a minute and then shook hands. "You didn't tell me that you were bringing a wife down. Are you trying to give me a heart attack old man? You really married this lovely young lady. I can hardly believe it. Welcome to Alaska, Mrs. Sweeny. Hope you enjoy the fishing experience. I take it that you are a Cheechako since he evidently brought you back from Los Angeles. He said he had a surprise for me when he called last week and said he was coming down, but I'd say it was more of a shock. The star bachelor has fallen!"

Josh had warned her that his friends would have a hard time believing that he was married and Josh was right.

Chapter 17

Watching the Dip Netters

Josh borrowed Kirk's pickup and the four climbed into the vehicle and were on their way. They drove down to the inlet, onto the sand and drove until they joined the other parked vehicles. Josh and Lonnie carried big nets while Beth and Candice each carried an ice chest to hold the fish and some snacks to snack on later. The first thing Beth noticed was fish heads all over the sand. Ugh! What an ugly sight that was.

"Why do they leave all these ugly fish heads on the beach? Why don't they throw them out in the ocean or something? They look awful!"

"If they throw them out there, they would just catch them back in their nets. Just watch and you'll see why," Josh suggested. "Besides, Beth, they will all wash away with the tide in the morning."

Before going out into the water, the three put on wetsuits. They looked a little funny with the suits and funny shoes, but that was what they had to do to keep from getting wet. Beth watched, fascinated. The three dip netters took their nets and went out into the inlet with the other dip netters. Beth watched as Josh came right back in with a big salmon in his net. She stood up and jumped up and down. "You got one," she exclaimed as she looked at the big wonderful salmon. "Put this salmon in the ice chest," he suggested.

"Oh, here comes Lonnie with one. Do you keep them separated?"

"No, we just put them all together," Candice explained.

"How many can you get?" Beth asked.

"Well the men are allowed twenty salmon apiece and their spouses fifteen," Candice answered.

Beth's mouth dropped open as she stared at Candice. "What ever would you do with all those salmon?" she asked.

"We don't get that many. We might take home twenty or so between us. Some we cut into fillets and freeze them, one or two we might leave whole so we can barbecue them in the back yard. The rest of them we can up for winter use. You can make a tasty salmon dip or salmon soup and even salmon casserole with canned salmon. It even makes good salmon sandwiches or salmon loaf. There's a salmon recipe book that Josh has that tells you lots of different ways to use your canned salmon. Some people who have dogs to feed take all the salmon they're allowed. But we take only what we'll eat through the year."

"Well, Josh must have run out of salmon as I haven't had one salmon fillet to eat yet!" stated Beth.

"Believe me, tonight you will have all the salmon you want to eat. Well, I need to get back out there and catch another one. How many do we have now?"

"It looks like about five and here come the men in with some more. Oh, look, Josh has two fish in his net. Oh, this is so much fun." Beth looked around at all the people dip netting. They were standing right next to each other. She wondered how in the world they could catch anything with so many other people dip netting. She tried to count the dip netters. Beth looked across the water and saw more dip netters on the other side. There were hundreds of people out in the inlet dip netting for some salmon to take home. It was all so fascinating.

About that time something whizzed past her head. What was that? Then another came almost right at her and she ducked. What on earth was going on? She backed way up out of the way. When Beth glanced around she realized that two women were throwing fish heads at each other and yelling at the top of their lungs. She couldn't understand a word they were saying. She just watched dumbfounded.

Josh came over and put his arm around his upset wife. "Don't worry about all this. You look so pale, Beth. This is something that happens now and then."

"Why? Why are they throwing fish heads at each other? Ugh! It's such a terrible thing that two women would do something like this."

"Both women think the salmon that's on the sand belong to their husband. The husbands will come out of the water and settle the arguments as soon as they notice them throwing the fish heads. With all the water moving and the men talking to each other, they haven't noticed their wives fighting as yet. Just sit back and enjoy the show."

"Yeah, enjoy the show. They only missed me by inches. If one of those fish heads had hit me, ooh. I would have died," Beth exclaimed.

"No, you would have fish blood all over you and a bump on the head, but that's it. Just stay away from those two, sit down on the sand and drink a cup of coffee or hot chocolate and forget it. You were enjoying all of this up to this time. Go back to having fun and think how funny those two women really are. It's a little on the ridiculous side."

"You're right. It is funny. I've never seen anything like that?"

"Do you realize how many times you use that phrase, Beth?"

"I know, but there's no other way to express it."

Josh went back to dip netting. This time all the fishermen were walking with their nets up the inlet about a block or so. Then they walked back on the sand and started all over again. Sometimes they had a fish in the net and other times they didn't. An older gentleman was sitting close to her so she asked him.

"Why are they walking now instead of standing still," Beth asked.

"The tide is coming in now and it's easier to catch the salmon walking as the fish swim toward the river."

"Oh," Beth said. She didn't know too much about tides. She visited with the gentleman for some time. It seems he had been an Alaskan for years.

"What do you like about Alaska?" Beth asked.

"About everything," he answered. "One thing is how good Alaska is to its senior citizens. We don't have to pay taxes on our houses or vehicles. And we don't have to buy a fishing license or a hunting license. It saves us quite a bit of money. They also have the permanent fund up here and that's nice to get. The permanent fund supplements our retirement income. It helps to get the proper clothing for Alaska and the right vehicles to drive in the winter on icy roads."

"Permanent fund, what's that."

"It comes from oil revenues. All Alaskan residents can receive a permanent fund. It varies every year in the amount you get. It's usually over a thousand dollars per resident. You have to be a resident for a year before you can apply. I take it you haven't been here a year yet."

"No, I haven't. But I'm going to talk with my husband and asked him about it. I'm sure he puts in for it every year. It's just one of the many things I'm learning about Alaska," Beth replied.

"Here comes my wife and it looks like she's been successful. She has a fish." The gentleman stood up and walked over to his wife. A boy about twelve years old followed. He took the fish for his grandpa and carried it over to where the grandfather cleaned the fish.

"My name is Tom and this is my grandson, Ryan, and my wife, Linda."

"It's nice to meet you, Tom. Hello Ryan." She looked at the grandmother who sat down on a chair to rest a bit. Beth had watched her dip netting walking up the inlet and noticed a lot of fishermen were passing her up as she slowly made her way up the inlet. She couldn't keep up with them. Finally, she got up and started again. She had a long ways to walk down to the sand before going back into the water.

"Grandma, you might just as well forget it. By the time you get down to the water, the tide will have changed," grinned the grandson.

Grandma cast him a stern look and said, "Everyone's a comedian." The woman slowly sauntered on down the sand.

When the grandma left, Beth asked, "Why does she work so hard at this? Do you need the fish that much? She looks so tired."

"No, we don't. I catch plenty of salmon off the shore on the Kenai River. She just loves to dip net. Linda's been dip netting for years and loves it. One of these days, she'll no longer be able to do it. I enjoyed it when I could, but now I'm too crippled up.

My grandson is just visiting us from outside and so he can't even go out in the water to help her. But as long as she enjoys it, I'll bring her. She's very careful and never goes out too far. It's too easy to lose your balance when a big wave hits you."

As Linda carefully stepped back in the water, Beth watched her. She was enjoying herself. Before she returned to where her husband was sitting, she had another salmon in her net and came lugging it toward them. It was evident that it was hard for her to carry the salmon. Ryan ran to help his grandmother.

"Tom, I think this is about all for today," Linda said and sat down in the chair exhausted.

"Okay," Tom said. He cleaned the fish and began gathering his belongings and the fish and headed for their vehicle. "It was nice to meet you, Beth, and I hope we see you again. I enjoyed our visit," he said as he left.

"Thank you for all the good Alaska information you gave me. I hope we see you next July when we come back again. My husband tells me they make this trip down here every year." Beth watched the three of them as they departed to their vehicle. What an interesting man Tom was. Too bad he was a little crippled up.

Beth watched some of the other dip netters until she saw Josh coming towards her. He explained that the group decided to get an extra five fish since they had another person to feed this year. After they had the twenty-five fish, they took out the cutting board and Beth watched the two men carry the cutting board down to the water. They cut the heads off the fish and let them drift along with the tide. They cleaned the fish and washed them real good in the water. When that was done, they loaded them into the coolers that they had lugged down to the shore from their vehicle.

"I almost hate to leave," Beth exclaimed. "This had been so much fun. Next year I'll get to dip net. Candice, what does it feel like when you get a salmon in your net? I think I would probably scream."

"It's always exciting to me. It startles you at first and then you are pleased and want to hurry and get to shore before the fish jump out unless they are really caught in the net. People often lose them before they get them to the shore."

"They sure are big salmon. I've never seen such big fish before. They are rather pretty too. Look at the coloring."

"Everything is bigger and better in Alaska, including the salmon," remarked Lonnie with his usual ornery grin.

"I know. I heard that before," laughed Beth.

"Let's head back to the motor home. It's still early and this evening we'll go salmon fishing. You do get to go salmon fishing," Josh explained. "I wished you could have dip netted with us, but there's next year."

"Oh, I had a nice time watching and visiting with my new friend Tom and his grandson. I really enjoyed talking with him. He was telling me about the permanent fund."

"I forgot to tell you about that. Too many things to remember to get my wife up to speed about Alaska," he explained. "Are you ready to throw your line in the water and fish for a big sockeye?"

"I want to catch a salmon not a sockeye. But I don't understand. With all the fish we already have, why are fishing for more?" the puzzled wife asked.

"You'll be surprised how fast the salmon go this winter. Besides, we'll can several of the salmon tonight or tomorrow. I brought the pressure cooker and some jars. The rest we'll fillet and put in the freezer in Kirk's house and then in the motor home freezer or coolers with ice until we get home. When we catch the halibut, we'll do the same. We'll can some and fillet some for the freezer. Believe me, they will taste good when winter comes and you get hungry for a big piece of salmon or halibut."

It did feel good to Beth to get back to the motor home and relax on the divan. She was a little tired after all that walking on the sand and carrying a bunch of salmon and equipment. But she had had a good day. Next year she had every intention of joining the three of them in the dip netting. Since everyone was a little tired, they decided to save the salmon fishing until tomorrow. They would can some salmon tonight after dinner. Dinner consisted of fried salmon, baked potatoes and a salad. Beth wasn't sure if she had ever tasted anything as good as the "red salmon" she had just eaten. They explained to her that the pink salmon were called humpies, the red salmon were called sockeye, and silver salmon were called coho.

Beth paid a lot of attention when they canned the fish. It was interesting and she was determined that she would do the canning the next time. She watched as they placed the filled jars into the pressure cooker. Then they processed it for a full 100 minutes. The canning process took up the whole evening, but finally all the fish were canned or filleted and frozen. Tomorrow all the fish would be frozen.

The four of them were up early in the morning and headed for the river. Beth was expecting that this would be something like trout fishing. Josh fixed her pole and showed her how to do the Kenai drag with the pole. This was different type of fishing for the new salmon fisherwoman. After a few times of throwing out her line and letting it drift down the river, she finally got the hang of it.

"The reds don't bite your hook, Beth. You let your line go drifting downstream hoping that it will hook a red salmon that comes up the stream with its mouth open. You keep trying and you'll get one sooner or later. If anything on your line feels different, just give it a quick jerk and hope it is a red salmon."

Beth tried over and over and nothing happened. Josh pulled one in and then another one. Both Candice and Lonnie had two each. Finally, Beth felt a jerk on her line and she had a fish on. She started to reel. This wasn't like trout fishing at all. It was hard work. The trout had been so easy to reel in. Beth kept reeling the best she could.

"Want some help, Cheechako?" asked Lonnie.

"No thanks! I can handle this job all by myself." If he hadn't been so ornery about it she would have accepted help; but after calling her a Cheechako, she was determined to do it herself. Finally she pulled the red salmon up on the shore. Her first salmon and it was a big one. Oh, how much fun and work that was.

While they were at the river bank, they cut the fish into fillets and put them in the ice chest. When they returned to the motor home, they would put the fillets into the freezer. They had each caught their limit of three fish. Some of the fishermen along the river said they often raise the limit of reds to six fish if the sockeye are plentiful.

The salmon fillets were all ready for the freezer except for a good washing in clean water rather than the river. It wouldn't take long to put them in food saver bags and then into the freezer.

Lonnie suggested that they have a quiet evening to prepare for the halibut fishing tomorrow. They would need to get up very early in the morning, he explained. It was an hour and a half drive to Homer and then it takes more time to back the boat into the water and get ready to go out in the bay.

"Beth, that means you must be up and ready to leave at five o'clock in the morning," explained Josh.

"Five?"

"You got it. That's ready to go so decide how long it will take you to get ready and plan to get up that much time before five."

"Wake me up at 4:30," she said and grimaced. Four-thirty wasn't even a civilized time of day.

Beth thanked Kirk for letting them use his boat. Kirk quickly explained that he and Josh had purchased the boat together with the understanding that when Josh came down, the boat would be available. Beth was thinking about this small boat that they would hardly have room to move around in little lone carry the halibut back. But when she saw the boat, she changed her mind. It was plenty big enough for the five of them.

Kirk encouraged her to climb into the boat and look around. With her curious nature she was only too happy to do exactly that. Glancing around the boat, she noticed steps leading down under the top of the boat. She slowly stepped down the steps and looked around. There was a small kitchenette that could be used to cook lunch. Also she noticed a very small bathroom. Beth was relieved to know that there was a bathroom on board. She had intended on drinking nothing so she wouldn't be stuck out on the ocean with no place to go, literally. Oh, this was going to be fun. She could hardly wait for the halibut trip in the morning.

Chapter 18

Halibut Fishing

At 4:30 in the morning, Beth rolled out of bed and had some toast and coffee. Josh gave her a pill to take. "If you take it now you won't get seasick. Since this is your first time on a boat, I believe it will be in your best interest to take this pill to insure you won't get seasick. There's nothing fun about being seasick and stuck out in the middle of the ocean and laying around all day heaving every now and then."

"You won't believe this, Hon, but I'm going to take your advice and swallow the pill," Beth said and proceeded to do so.

Josh tried not to look shocked. "She's finally learning," he thought. She had learned so many things the hard way and he didn't want her to learn about seasickness the hard way. He sighed a sigh of relief. He didn't tell her that he was going to insist that she take the pill and he was glad he didn't have to. He'd never pushed his wife to that point and he didn't want to now.

Kirk knocked on the motor home door and heard four voices say, "Come in."

"My wife has to work but I'm free today. Do you suppose you could find a place for me to fish on the boat?" asked Kirk. "Alice is not too happy thinking about me going fishing without her but she couldn't get the day off."

"Be glad to have you, my friend. That means you are the boat driver and I get more fishing time. Everyone get your gear together and let's get on our way. Beth, take the warm jacket as you never know what the weather will be when you're out on the water. I called my friend in Homer and he said the weather was good. Let's hope it stays that way all day." Josh headed for the boat.

It was a little crowded in the pickup, but they made it and enjoyed the fellowship all the way down to Homer. It was only a little over an hour and a half before they were at Homer and stopped at a rest stop. Beth was again taken back at the scenery. Trees, blue, blue skies, moose running here and there, and many more interesting sights all the way to Homer.

The men backed the boat into the water by the wharf and then Kirk drove the truck and boat trailer up to the parking lot and was soon hurrying back down the boat ramp. He released the ropes that held the boat to the ramp and climbed into the boat with the other prospective halibut fisherpersons. Finally, they were slowly drifting out of the marina to reach the Kachemac Bay. They were on their way to a specific place that Kirk and Josh knew was good halibut fishing.

The halibut trip that Beth had heard of for many months was now under way. The water was smooth and the weather perfect. She had intended to stay down in the kitchen area but it was too nice out and she didn't want to miss anything.

The whole area was beyond description to the new Alaskan. It was breathtaking. The mountains surrounding the inlet made the whole scene so perfect. Beth took out her digital camera and began to snap pictures. She had a camera that took action pictures so it didn't matter if the birds or animals moved she still got good pictures even if she moved a little while shooting. Beth had informed her husband that if she caught a halibut, he had to take her picture while she brought it in and he agreed. Beth was surprised at how long it was taking to reach the designated fishing area, but she was enjoying the boat ride.

Finally they arrived at a place where the fish finder indicated that there were fish below. Josh fixed her pole first and showed her how to lower the fish line into the water. He told her to make sure that she kept the line on the bottom, moving it once in a while. Josh explained that the boat drifted and often she would find that her line was not on the bottom. Beth lifted her pole from time to time to make sure she could feel the sinker hit the bottom of the inlet. That's where the halibut were according to her four fishing companions.

She was half daydreaming as she moved her pole up just a little when something went wrong. She tried to reel but it was so hard she couldn't make the line move much. "I think I've caught a rock or something on the bottom as I can barely move the reel. What do I do now?"

"Beth, see how your line is moving? A rock doesn't do that. Reel your line in, you have a fish on. It's hard, but reel the best you can."

"I'm reeling but it seems to go out faster than I can real it in."

Kirk piped up, "Hey, Cheechako, want some help reeling that in?"

"I'll manage just fine, I think."

"Let me have your pole for a minute, Beth." Josh pulled the pole up and started reeling and then set the pole in the holder and reeled some more. "Now, Hon, just keep reeling. It will be easer for you this way."

"You're right, it is easier." She noticed that the other four people had reeled their poles in and were watching her. She assumed it was because they might tangle up with her line as her halibut kept moving around. Finally, she gave out and asked Josh to reel for a while. Josh did and it was even hard for him to reel. At least it isn't only me, she thought. It seemed to be forever before Josh brought the fish up close enough to the top of the water so they could gaff it and pull it into the boat.

Kirk was right there along with Lonnie and the three men pulled it in. "This halibut must weigh 100 pounds," exclaimed Kirk. "Talk about beginners luck, that Cheechako evidently has it."

That was about the first time that Beth was proud of being a Cheechako. She started to get closer and noticed that the fish was bouncing all over the place trying to get free. Josh and Kirk both took a few swats on their legs from its tail before they were able to subdue the halibut and put it out of its misery. Beth did all she could do to keep from laughing at the scene and then she spied Candice who was bent over laughing at the three men and halibut circus.

The halibut was too big for the fishing well so they put it to one side of the boat out of the way. Candice and Lonnie had already lowered their lines into the water and started fishing. Beth could hardly wait to put her pole back in the water. She knew it wasn't her fishing skill that caught the halibut—it was just plain luck. But she couldn't help smiling to herself to think that she had caught the first one and a good size one at that. She had thought the salmon were big fish, but they were small compared to this halibut.

Beth heard a holler and saw both Lonnie and Candice reeling for all they were worth. They either both had a halibut or they had one between the two and it had tangled into the other one's line. Once the line was partly untangled, it turned out that the halibut was on Lonnie's line.

So Beth sat back down and waited to see what happened next. Finally the two pulled up one fish with lots of tangled line. It was only about half the size of hers but she said nothing and tried hard to keep from smiling.

The new halibut fisherwoman put her line back into the water. This time she put it in the fish holder and just pulled the line up and down once in a while to make sure it was on the bottom. All of a sudden she had another fish on. But it wasn't as hard to reel in. Must be an awful small halibut compared to her last one. She reeled it up easily and as the men pulled it out of the water, she gasped.

"What is that horrible looking fish?" she exclaimed.

"It's called an Irish lord. He's rather good looking. Congratulations, you are the first one that caught one. Do you want to keep him?" Kirk asked.

She glanced at Josh and knew by his grin that Kirk was teasing her. "I think I'll let you have this one since you aren't having any luck fishing," she said without a smile. That had to be the ugliest fish there ever was. The big head and ugly bug-eyes made the fish so horrible looking, she couldn't believe anything could look that bad.

"Before I put this fish back into the water, don't you want to have your picture taken with it?" Kirk asked.

"No!" she said quickly.

Beth was relieved when Kirk threw the Irish lord back into the water. She was looking out over the water when she asked excitedly, "What kind of animal is that? It's swimming on its back. Oh look, there a baby on its stomach. He's so cute." She picked up her camera and took a fast shot.

"That's a sea otter. They come pretty close to the boats at times, but keep a safe distance. Almost every time we come halibut fishing, we find several different families of sea otters. If you look over there a little further, you'll see a lot of them. They seem to travel in families. If you do see one alone, you just wait a while or look around and you usually see a lot more. They are plentiful here in this bay," Kirk explained.

"Hey, Beth, look at the front of the boat a little distance away. There's a beluga whale. Get your camera ready and try to snap him when he comes out of the water or spews water," Josh said. Beth took as many pictures as she could until Josh started reeling. Here's another halibut, she thought.

Josh was reeling hard now and had a fish on so she waited until he brought his safely in the boat. It was a nice one. It wasn't as big as hers, but close. He looked happy as he and Kirk gaffed the halibut and brought it on board. Beth decided that they must have found a real halibut-fishing hole. He had no sooner had his fish in the boat when everyone threw their lines back in the water. Kirk was the next one to reel in a fish and a nice one.

Beth felt another tug on her line and started reeling again. It was hard, but not as hard as before. But it didn't feel like another Irish lord. The line was wiggling like the first halibut. Sure enough she had caught another halibut about half the size of the first one. She was happy.

"Well, Cheechako, now you have to quit fishing," Kirk remarked.

"Why?"

"You can only catch two halibut. You caught your two."

"Can't I help my husband catch his two?"

"I don't think you're going to get a chance. He looks like he's pulling his second one in right now and Candice is pulling in one as well on the other side of the boat. Just sit and relax and enjoy the action and the view."

Was he serious? Did she really have to quit fishing? She barely got started, she thought. But she looked at her watch. It was two o'clock already. Where had the time gone? Maybe she should go fix some coffee or tea or some snack or something, but she hated to miss anything. Candice no sooner brought her halibut on board when Lonnie had one on and she noticed that Kirk was reeling as hard as he could to bring his second halibut on board. When Kirk's halibut was gaffed and put in the fishing well, he started baiting his line again.

Beth stepped up. "You've caught your two. Put your pole away," she ordered.

Kirk cracked up. "I just wanted to see what you would do if I dropped my line back into the water. I really wasn't going to let my line down. You're one easy Cheechako to tease." Kirk looked at the halibut in the fishing well. "I think we're only missing one fish and we'll all have to relax and let Candice catch her last one."

As the four successful fisher people sat and relaxed while watching Candice fish, they were also enjoying a soda and a snack as well as the view and the fellowship. It had been a good day, Beth thought. In about ten minutes, Candice pulled in the last halibut. They were going home with ten halibut between all of them. It was definitely a successful trip.

Before leaving Homer, they pulled into the parking lot by a restaurant and had a snack lunch. "Don't eat too much folks, because I have an idea that Alice will have dinner all ready when we get home and she'll be a little upset if none of us want to eat her dinner."

It was now three-thirty and everyone was hungry. Beth did her best to just snack a little, but she felt as though she could eat a full-blown meal easily. She had snacked on the boat and that helped.

Beth had every intention of watching the scenery on the way back to Soldotna, but she laid her head back and closed her eyes just for a moment when someone started shaking her. "We're back in Soldotna, Beth, you have to wake up." It was Candice trying to wake her. Candice was barely awake herself.

When they drove into Kirk's driveway shortly, Kirk made an announcement. "Now, Cheechako, everyone has to carry their halibut into the garage to be cleaned. We'll take your smaller one, but that big one is up to you."

Kirk never stopped teasing her. She walked over to the fish and looked at it. Over a hundred pounds and she was supposed to pick that halibut up and carry it into the garage. She thought not. "I think you're just jealous because I caught a bigger one than you. So therefore, I'm going to let you have the privilege of carrying my halibut into the garage and then you'll know how it feels to carry a big halibut," she said and smiled as she walked into the house with Candice.

When the two stepped into the house, they found Alice with dinner on the table waiting for them. The men would water down the fish and be right in. Normally they cleaned the fish at Homer but they wanted pictures of the halibut, so they brought them home to clean.

After the delicious dinner was eaten, they all went to work on the halibut—that is after the pictures were taken. Although

Beth couldn't lift her fish, the men strung it up for her and she stood beside it. Kirk had weighed it and it weighed 110 pounds. He told her the halibut would have weighed a little more if weighed right out of the water.

It didn't take long for the men to clean the halibut. The ladies made fillets out of some of the halibut and sealed them in food saver bags. The packages were put in Kirk and Alice's freezer until the four of them started home to Fairbanks. The rest of the halibut was canned. Beth was fascinated with the way the men cut up the halibut. There were actually lines on the halibut that showed you where to cut. She just knew she would be able to cut up a halibut—it looked so easy. There sure was a lot more of the meat that was good on a halibut than on the salmon. Only the head and tale were thrown away along with a few halibut guts and the backbone.

Beth was amazed how much her halibut actually made. Package after package from just the one halibut made a big stack of fish fillets. Well if they ran out of everything else this coming winter, they could sure eat halibut. Josh had showed her his halibut cookbook that had all the different recipes in it. The recipes did sound good.

Chapter 19

Watching the Caribou

The next morning the four co-travelers decided they would do some sightseeing for Beth's sake. Lonnie, Candice and Josh had seen most of the Kenai Peninsula, but they wanted Beth to experience it as well. Kirk promised that Alice would have a dinner waiting for them around six o'clock. That sounded good to them.

"First Beth, I want us to go to Seward so we can show you the glacier," Josh explained. "It has melted a lot since we first saw the glacier some years ago, but it's still there. It will take about an hour and a half to get there but it's worth the drive. We'll stop at a few other places along the way. After viewing the glacier, we'll probably be ready to eat so we'll then have lunch in one of the Seward restaurants."

Lonnie spoke up. "There's a visitor's center, a museum, and an interesting fishery to see while we are there. We should be able to do all that before heading back so we can be in Soldotna by six o'clock. How much do you want to bet that we have halibut steaks for dinner?"

Beth smiled. She had tasted halibut only once before and that was at Alaska Land. She had almost forgotten how it tasted. Beth had heard a lot about how good it was and was anticipating having another bite of the big fish. "Halibut steaks sound good to me," she said. Then Beth thought about what Josh said. "Does every place we want to go take over an hour to get there? It was over an hour to Homer and now you say over an hour to Seward. Where else do we go for over an hours ride on this peninsula?"

"It's true that you have to do a little driving here on the peninsula. That's for sure. Once you've been to Homer and Seward that means that you'll have seen the bulk of the Kenai Peninsula. There is a Captain Cook Park we could go see, but it's mostly scenery and I think you've seen a lot of that on the trip to Homer. Captain Cook Park is right by the ocean and rather nice to visit."

"Isn't there a town or something named Kenai also? I've only seen Soldotna and Homer," Beth remarked.

"Yes, and we'll drive over there tomorrow and go looking for caribou. They are certainly different animals than the moose. Some of their racks are bigger than the animals are," Lonnie explained.

"Beth, the caribou are what you and I would call elegant. They are somewhat better looking than the moose," Candice said.

"What will we do with the rest of the week?" Beth asked.

"We have to go clam digging. We might want to take two days for clam digging. They say the tide is good for clams the day after tomorrow. So we'll plan on doing that. In the meantime we'll see Seward today."

Everywhere she looked, Beth was amazed at the views. Never had she seen anything like this. There was a blue-green clear river flowing between two mountains. The mountains were colored with different bushes and trees as well as different shaped rocks. A few wild flowers were blooming as far as she could see up the mountains. Alaska had to have the best scenery anywhere in the world.

When they arrived at the glacier park, Beth was more than ready to get out of the pickup. They stopped at the little refreshment store and each bought a soda and started on the long walk to the glacier. Even here was beautiful scenery. It did take some time to get to the glacier but it was worth it. They walked down to where the glacier water forms a stream. "Put your hand in the stream, Beth," suggested Lonnie.

"Why?"

"Just so you can check the temperature of the water."

"You first."

Lonnie reached down and put his hand in the water and pulled it out like there was nothing to it. Beth followed suit but pulled her hand out in a hurry.

"That's cold ice water in that stream."

"How cold do you think it is?" laughed Lonnie.

"Cold enough, that's how cold it is."

Beth loved the glacier and the huge snow pile. It had a blue color to it and made a good picture. She was glad she brought that extra chip for her camera. They walked up the trail a ways to get closer to the glacier. Finally, they started back to their vehicle. Josh pointed out all the different places where the glacier used to be through the years. It was hard to believe that the glacier actually was that large at one time many years back. It was big enough now, as far as she was concerned.

When they drove through Seward, they drove right up as far as the road would go and right by the inlet. People were in boats fishing and some standing along the side of the bank fishing. They were so close together that Beth couldn't see how their lines didn't get tangled up. This must be what that postcard was all about that showed people fishing so close and written on the card was, "combat fishing." That certainly looked like combat fishing to her. She was glad there weren't quite that many people fishing when she fished for salmon in the Kenai River.

The four stopped at the museum and enjoyed seeing all the different artifacts that were displayed. There were lots of artifacts that once belonged to Eskimos and Indians. They spent considerable time viewing the early Alaskan belongings.

Then they headed for a restaurant. Beth looked at the halibut dishes on the menu but decided she could wait until dinner to taste halibut again. She ordered a big bowl of clam chowder along with a ham sandwich. She wondered if all food in Alaska tasted good because she was in Alaska. Beth made a remark about how good food tasted since she came to Alaska.

"We told you, Beth, that everything is bigger and better in Alaska," Lonnie said with his usual teasing grin.

After visiting a few tourist shops, they decided it was time to head for Soldotna. It had been an interesting day in Seward. Beth bought a few little things, but didn't see anything particular she really wanted.

True to his word, Kirk and Alice had dinner all ready. After the long drive they were ready for a nice quiet dinner.

"Tonight we have some halibut waiting for you," Alice declared. "I have my own special recipe and it is good even if I have to say so myself."

"I agree that with that statement," Kirk added.

Beth so enjoyed the halibut. It was absolutely delicious. She wondered if she would be able to make it taste that good. It sure was different than other fish. More delicate, she thought.

There would be one more day of sight seeing. They were going to look for caribou and whatever wildlife they might find. At nine o'clock the next morning, the sightseers left for Kenai. Josh pointed out the nice nurseries along the way. Soon they came to a stop sign and turned right on Bridge Access Road. Beth could see a bridge that crossed over the Kenai River, but before they came to the bridge, they saw some caribou in the tundra. In fact there were a good many caribou milling around in the tundra. Josh pulled the pickup off the road to the left side where there was room to park.

"I want to get closer to the caribou so I can get a good picture," Beth exclaimed. She stepped out of the car and walked across the road to the very edge. The road was built up so the caribou were down the road base a few feet and not too close to the road.

They studied the caribou. Beth couldn't figure out how they could stand up with their racks so big. The racks actually looked taller than the animal itself.

One big old male wasn't too far away. "Now hold right still and look this way," Beth told him. And as if he knew what she said, he stood and posed for her. When she turned back to go across the road, she couldn't. The traffic had piled up going both ways watching the caribou and now were moving slowly.

Beth could do nothing until the long line of cars moved past her on both sides of the road. All at once the big caribou whose picture she had taken decided he wanted to cross the road. All cars stopped both ways and Beth walked across the road with her caribou friend albeit several feet away from the caribou. It was almost as though he knew she needed to go across the road. Beth was dumbfounded to say the least. He couldn't really know he was helping her get back to her automobile on the other side of the road but that's exactly what he did.

Finally, after an hour or so taking pictures of the caribou and watching them, the sightseers decided to move on to Kenai. The four stopped at the Kenai Visitor Center and again enjoyed the articles and pictures of early Alaska. Finally they drove on out Marathon Road to look for more animals. However, after driving out there, they found nothing. It seemed that most of the caribou had gone to the tundra by Bridge Access Road.

As they drove back to Kenai, the ladies decided they wanted to stop at one of the tourist stores and look around. They shopped in three different shops before they decided it was time to eat. Kirk had advised them to try his favorite restaurant. He was right. They had a good lunch at Paradisio's.

That evening Alice again had dinner ready. They were getting spoiled with all the good dinners she had provided for them.

Chapter 20

Clam Digging

Beth yawned the next morning, trying to wake up. So this was the day they would go clam digging, whatever that was. After breakfast she watched Kirk take a bag of cornmeal and put it in the pickup. That's strange, she thought. Do you catch clams with cornmeal—surely not? She wasn't about to ask.

Josh was loading all the wet suits into the car. They were the ones they used when they went dip netting for salmon. Did they go out in the water to get the clams? She sure felt dumb. She would ask no questions and just watch what was going on and follow suit.

Finally the four of them were on their way to Clam Gulch. It looked to Beth that they were headed for Homer again. "Is this a long drive?"

"No only about forty-five minutes or little less," Lonnie answered.

"Did you say, Beth, that you'd never been clam digging before?" asked Candice.

"That's right. I have no idea what I'm getting into. But I'm game. If you three can dig clams, I'm sure I can."

"You enjoyed the halibut fishing, didn't you?"

"Oh, yes. It was so much fun. I would love to go again, but I guess we have about all the halibut we can eat this coming year."

"Thanks to you, we do have all we need," Candice agreed. "The trouble is finding another good day to go halibut fishing before we leave for home. I overheard the men talking and I think they want to do a little more salmon fishing and this time they want to go to Sterling. They have friends there and want to visit with them while they are fishing."

"That sounds good to me. Didn't we pass Sterling on our way to Seward?"

"Yeah, it's one of those places if you blinked your eyes you'll miss it. There aren't a lot of stores in Sterling but there are a lot of people who live there," Candice remarked.

"For someone who never did any fishing before coming to Alaska, I'm sure getting a good dose of it now. I'm beginning to understand why Josh was so exited about coming down here to the peninsula. He was like a little kid," she whispered to Candice.

"Hang on, Beth, we are about to turn into Clam Gulch. We'll drive right down this gravel road and onto the beach and up just a ways to get out of the crowd. It's a minus five tide and that means it's a good time to dig clams. You'll love it, just wait and see."

Carefully, Josh drove the pickup down the winding road watching out for all the walkers who shared the road with the cars. Once they were at the bottom, Josh put the pickup in four-wheel-drive and up the beach they went. Finally, he parked the pickup and everyone piled out of the vehicle.

Lonnie handed out the wetsuits to everyone and they began pulling them over their clothes. When he handed Beth one, she wasn't sure that she wanted to put on the ugly outfit. Josh came over and stood by her.

"You have to get down on the ground in the wet sand and dig for clams. Do you want your slacks to get muddy? If not, just put on this wetsuit. That way you can enjoy the sand so much more. Also use these plastic gloves and that will help save you from getting a few cuts from the clams."

"The clams cut you or bite you?"

Candice and Lonnie quickly walked away to keep from laughing.

"The shells on the clams are sharp. Sometimes you reach for a clam and cut yourself. These thin plastic gloves help a lot to avoid that. It also prevents a lot of sand from getting under your fingernails."

Beth put on the wetsuit. It really didn't feel too bad. Then she put on the boots that went along with it. The day was nice and she had on a sweatshirt and was plenty warm. Josh suggested that she take her hat if she didn't want to get sunburned. "It's twice as bad with the sun and the reflection on the water. Besides you look cute in that hat. You look like a baseball player."

Everyone was given a bucket and a clam shovel. They headed out toward the ocean waves. After going almost to the waves, Josh stopped. He came over to Beth and showed her the little dimples in the sand. "Watch," he said. Josh began digging an inch from the dimple. One big scoop and he reached down and picked up a clam.

Beth's eyes bugged as she eyed the clam. It was a funny looking creature with its neck sticking out of the shell but it was a very interesting creature.

Josh grabbed her hand. "Here, Beth. This one has its neck

stuck out of the ground. Just take your thumb and forefinger and push tight and then pull on it hard. It should come right out." Beth did.

"Oh, I caught one, my first clam. Where's the camera?"

Josh dutifully took the camera out of his shirt pocket and let her hold onto the clam and took her picture. He had always enjoyed his trip to the Kenai Peninsula, but with Beth along it was double the fun. She was a character and loved to have new experiences. He had to admit that his wife was a good sport.

Beth saw a dimple and dug a hole and tried to find the clam. But there was nothing in the hole. "Okay, what did I do wrong?"

"You waited too long. As soon as that clam feels the shovel digging, it takes off and digs deeper. So you have to be quick. Here, you get down on your knees. That's good. See this dimple? I'll dig and you reach in real quick and grab the clam." He dug and she grabbed.

"Oh that works well. Dig another hole." It worked so well that the two decided to work together and get their limit of clams. It was such a good day for clam digging that the four of them had their limit in two hours.

Beth wasn't in any hurry to return to the truck. She loved the beach and just wanted to go for a walk. The air smelled so good. She took the camera from Josh and started snapping pictures of the scenery and the clam diggers and anything of interest she could find.

As they walked back to the truck, Beth said to her husband, "I'm not ready to leave the beach, but I guess we have to. It's just so nice here. I love the smell of the ocean and the whole area. It's good to be here."

"You're right, it is good to be here. We'll be here a little longer. We want to stop at the creek and wash the clams and cover them with water and cornmeal."

"Let me get this straight. You are going to cover the clams with cornmeal. I saw Kirk putting the cornmeal in the truck and wondered why. Can I ask why you are putting cornmeal on the clams without sounding too dumb?"

"Beth, none of your questions are dumb. You're new to all of this. Don't worry so much about asking dumb questions. We put the cornmeal over the clams, quite a bit of cornmeal. Clams dig through sand and they have sand all through them and it's hard to get the sand out. The clams will dig through the cornmeal eating it and that will clean the sand out of them and it's much easier to prepare the clams for canning or for clam chowder. It saves a lot of time cleaning clams, believe me." Josh was looking at Beth as she smiled and nodded her head.

"Why are you smiling?" he asked.

"I don't think you want to know. I had my own idea why he brought the cornmeal along and now it sounds perfectly stupid."

"You thought we would catch the clams with cornmeal?"

"I didn't say that."

"But you thought that cause that's what I thought the first time I ever went clam digging," laughed Josh and hugged his wife.

They were at the truck now and everyone started taking off their wetsuits and boots and putting them in the pickup. It did feel good to get out of the heavy pants. They drove down the beach to the little creek they had passed over on the way to their clam site. The men grabbed the buckets of clams and rinsed them thoroughly and put them all in one big tub. Then they dumped the whole sack of cornmeal over the clams. They washed the shovels and buckets until the sand was removed and put them in the pickup.

"Well, ladies, time to go home," Lonnie said as he took the driver's position. After driving back up the dusty road, Lonnie stopped and took the pickup out of four-wheel-drive and was motioned to stop at the stop sign. There stood a game warden waiting for them.

"I need to see your license," he said and then looked at Josh. "Well, hello, Josh, it's been some time since I saw you. How are you doing?"

While taking out his wallet to get his license, he talked with the officer. "Good to see you, Ron. It has been a while. I missed you on the last trip. Ladies, do you have your licenses ready?" Josh handed them to Ron. Ron blinked and looked at Josh.

"Now, Josh, I know you don't have any sisters. This Elizabeth Sweeny couldn't possibly be your wife could she?"

Josh grinned at his friend. "It's my privilege to introduce you to my wife, Elizabeth Sweeny, better known as Beth."

Ron reached in and shook her hand. "It's a privilege to meet you. Talk about a shock, I can't believe it. We had all decided that Joshua Sweeny was never going to get married."

Ron looked at the clams in the back of the pickup. "Did you get your limit?"

"We sure did. Right on the dot, that is if we know how to count. It was a good day to clam dig—weather wise and clam wise. This was Beth's first time and she made a good clam digger."

"Cheechako?"

"Yes, that she is, but she's learning fast to be an Alaskan," Josh said as he grinned at his friend.

"I guess I better let you go. The cars are backing up and I'm supposed to check them all. Stop by the house if you get a chance. Be nice to visit with you," Ron said and waved them on.

Lonnie drove on the gravel road until he hit the highway and then headed for Soldotna. "What would you ladies prefer? You want to go to the drive-in and get a sandwich or do you want to go back to the motor home and make some type of a lunch?" asked Josh.

"What do you think, Beth?"

"I don't know. What sounds good to you?"

"I asked you first," Candice said.

"I'll stop at the nearest drive-in and we'll have sandwiches and sodas," Lonnie said. "You aren't going to get a straight answer out of those two. I think we worked them a little too hard."

"Worked them too hard," exclaimed Josh. "I had to do all the digging and Beth just sat down on the job. All she had to do was lift a tiny clam out now and then."

Beth glared at Josh. "Come to think of it, she did do a little bit of work at that," he admitted.

Beth smiled. She had never been teased much—a little during college years—but she sure had to learn to get used to it with these Alaskan friends. It was rather neat bickering back and forth just for the fun of it, she decided. The whole Alaskan experience had been great but some of the best times were right down here on the Kenai Peninsula, the new Alaskan decided.

When they arrived at the motor home, Lonnie suggested that they all take it easy for a while and then they would start the clam cleaning. The clams needed a little more time digesting the cornmeal to make sure they were cleaned out completely. If they waited for a while, sometimes the clams would open up and it was easier to get the meat out of the shell when they were open.

Chapter 21

The Floating Pickup

Both Candice and Beth had taken a short nap. Rested, the two were now ready to start in on the clams. Beth thought it would be a lot of fun. Cleaning fish hadn't been too bad once she got used to it.

"We're going to clean them systematically. Lonnie is going to open the clams and take out the meat. I'm going to cut off the bad part, and separate the foot from the rest of the clam. You ladies can clean the rest however you want," Josh instructed.

Grabbing the tub of clams, the two men carried it over to one side in the yard. They carefully rinsed the clams and Lonnie started opening them and dumping the meat in a pan. Beth gasped at the gross looking stuff that Josh cut off the clams. She wrinkled her nose. She didn't think she was going to be able to eat clams after seeing that horrible disgusting stuff that Josh cut off. But then the new clam digger remembered the inside of the fish wasn't exactly appetizing either.

But once Josh washed the clams again and the icky stuff was gone, the results looked much more appetizing to Beth. Now the ladies took the clam meat into the garage and started cleaning them. Kirk had his garage all set up for cleaning fish and clams so it made it an easier job with such a convenient cleaning table.

"I've found that if we wash and wash and wash the clams over and over, that gets what little sand and other things left on them. You take the necks and cut off the brown spot and then cut the neck open and I'll do the rest."

"That sounds good to me. This part looks a lot better than the part Josh cut off. That's absolutely gross. I was afraid I wouldn't be able to eat the clams, but this part looks much better."

It took two hours before all of the clams were cleaned, ground up, and put in jars to be canned. They did save some out for clam chowder for dinner and a few of the clam feet to fry and eat. This one time they were determined to have dinner all ready for Kirk and Alice. They would make a salad. Candice sent Lonnie to the store for some dessert and some crackers for the chowder. They would cook the clam chowder in the motor home and invite their friends to eat with them.

It was close to the time that Alice and Kirk would come home from work. They had everything for the dinner all finished. Alice welcomed the already cooked meal. She came right in the motor home and sat down.

"My turn to get waited on," she said. "It's been a hard day at work. Usually it's a good job, but now and then there are some disgruntled customers that want something for nothing and where do they send them? To me! So this dinner is a special treat and especially clam chowder. It's one of my favorite dishes."

The six of them ate every scrap of the clam chowder. Beth thought it was the best soup she had ever eaten. The restaurants didn't have anything that even compared to Josh's chowder. He was the one that was voted to cook it. With all the jars of clams they were taking home, she would make sure she made good use of them. Beth just bet the soup would taste even better this winter.

"So what's your plan for tomorrow?" asked Kirk.

"I wanted to go to Sterling and do a little fishing in my old fishing hole. We used to call it Smiley Rock because someone painted a smiley face on a rock. I think they eventually named it something else, but I can't remember what. We probably won't fish too long, but I'd like to show Beth around Sterling a little."

"Boy, that'll take all day," Kirk laughed.

"Well, just some of the scenery. It should be rather fun. It's a little different type fishing than all these places that have so many tourists."

The four had a good time visiting that evening and made their plans for the next day. Not until Beth finally lay down on her bed did she realize how tired she was. The bed did feel good. Josh, Kirk, and Lonnie were visiting still, but Candice and Beth decided it was bedtime.

The next thing Beth knew, someone was shaking her. "What, what's wrong?"

"It's time to get up. We need to go early in order to get my favorite fishing hole. Are you awake yet?"

"Just barely awake, but I'll be ready in minutes. What's for breakfast?"

"Toast and jam and coffee, is that okay?"

"That sounds good to me."

"The toast is all made and ready for you and so is the coffee. Just dress and get ready. Candice and Lonnie are already up and fed and waiting for us. You must have been very tired to sleep so hard not to hear them."

"I felt as though I had just slid into bed when you shook me."

Beth hurried as she dressed, brushed her teeth and barely washed up. She took her two pieces of toast in a napkin, carried a covered cup of coffee, and announced that she was ready to go. They had the pickup all loaded and were soon on their way.

When they drove down the gravel road several feet from the river, Josh parked the vehicle. It was then that he spotted his old friend Barry Burns just getting out of his pickup and heading for the river. The men were passing out the fishing poles to the ladies and getting their equipment ready when all at once Barry's old pickup moved and was heading for the river. It was too late for Josh or Lonnie to try to catch up with it and it just barely missed Barry as it drove itself right into the river.

A stunned Barry watched his vehicle go floating down the swift and very deep river that was in its peek this time of the year. Josh and Lonnie didn't know what to say. The two waited for Barry to say something. The truck-less man was still watching his pickup go sailing down the Kenai not believing what he saw.

"Any chance you folks could give me a ride home when you get ready?" asked the embarrassed fisherman. "I'm sure I set the break on the pickup, but then it is so old, it probably doesn't work like it should. I should have turned the steering wheel towards the bank, but the break has always worked before. The truck isn't worth much, but all the rest of my fishing gear is in that pickup. You wouldn't happen to have a few eggs or fly hooks or something I could fish with, would you, Josh?"

"Help yourself, Barry. By the time we noticed what was happening, the pickup was almost at the water's edge. I've seen lots of boats on the Kenai but never before have I seen someone sail their pickup down the river. To each his own they say."

Barry burst out laughing. "It was rather funny wasn't it? I saw that lady up there calling 911. She probably thinks someone might have been in the pickup. I need to wait around until the authorities come and explain to them what happened."

The fishermen and women found a good spot and started fishing again. After they caught a few fish, they saw a policeman drive down the gravel road and park. He stepped out of his vehicle and walked toward the fishermen.

"Whose pickup went into the river?" he asked.

"It's mine, sir," Barry said.

"Was anyone in the pickup?"

"Oh, no, sir, there was only my fishing equipment in the pickup."

"Tell me what happened," the policeman stated.

"I parked the pickup as I usually do and I remember setting the break, but for some reason it must not have held. It's an old pickup and I guess the hand break is worn out or something. It's never done this before but there's a first time for everything," Barry answered.

"I don't see a pickup anywhere in the river," the policeman commented sternly as he stared down the Kenai River trying to find something that looked different. If there was a pickup in that river, he sure didn't see it.

"Oh it went sailing right on down the river at a pretty good rate. I don't know where it will end up. It might get caught in some tree or something. We'll go looking pretty soon and see if we can find it," answered Barry.

"It won't do you much good to try to retrieve the vehicle now with the river all but at flood stage. Later in the fall the water will go down considerably and then you can probably rescue it, however, I'm not sure if it will be of any use to you. You might have a few salmon trapped in it not to mention all the other creatures that could find their way into you vehicle," smiled the officer.

The policeman proceeded to write down Barry's name and address and phone number. He said they would call if they found the pickup. He hoped it didn't sail on down the river and out to the ocean.

As the policeman drove up the gravel road, Barry smiled. "Real encouraging, that policeman saying my pickup might end up in the ocean. I believe it will end up where the river takes a good turn and the pickup will be lodge in the bushes there. But, I'm going to take his word and not worry about it until the river isn't quite so full."

Josh went over and stood by his friend. "Are you okay with all this?"

"Actually it's okay. It's not that that's my only vehicle. I have a new pickup at home but I loved driving the old wreck. But, now I'll have to drive the new one. Whenever you four are ready to go, I am. I have two fish and that's all we can take care of right now. We have our freezer full of salmon besides all the canned salmon. I'll probably give my neighbor one of these or have him over for a fish fry."

"Well, I'm ready. How about the rest of you? You ready to go to the restaurant and have a good breakfast or should I say brunch? None of us ate enough breakfast to last us very long. Say, Barry, you come along too and we'll treat you to breakfast for the all the entertainment that you gave us this morning," grinned Josh.

Barry returned the grin and the group crowded into the pickup and headed for the restaurant. Come to think of it, they were all hungry.

Chapter 22

Headed Home

The next morning the group reluctantly made the preparations to return to Fairbanks. Although Beth was anxious to be back in her own home, she had so enjoyed all of the experiences on the peninsula that she wasn't quite ready to go home.

On the way, Beth noticed all the stunted trees. She had meant to ask Josh about the trees before, but forgot. "Josh, how come there are so many trees that seem dwarfed? All over the place you see them. Then, again, you see normal trees. What's that all about?" she asked pointing at the miniature trees.

"They are growing in permafrost and therefore can't grow very fast or any larger than they are. The ground is frozen underneath and they can't get any food up to the tree. Some of them are a thousand years old. When people want to use some of the land, they have to dig down real deep and put a little gravel in there and fill it up with dirt that isn't frozen. It's quite a process and expensive, but then after all that work, the land is ready for building houses and growing gardens. Early pioneers built on the permafrost only to see their houses sink down a few feet when the warm weather came and thawed the ground. They soon learned not to build there unless they treated the land."

"That's interesting. I never heard of permafrost before but it does make sense. Okay, someone call me a Cheechako and get it over with," laughed Beth.

Josh made a stop when they reached the Chugach Forest. They drove into the park and just took some time looking around and resting a bit. There was a stream and Beth could see the salmon swimming in the stream.

Finally they were on the road once more. The view of the river was beautiful—a blue-green clear color. It didn't seem that one could find a clean and clear river like this in the lower forty-eight. When they came to Turnagain road, Beth wondered why they would call a road by that name. But then she guessed that the road turned and turned and then turned again. Probably that was where that name came from.

All at once, Josh pulled the motor home off the road. "Get your camera out, Beth, and start snapping pictures. See those bighorn sheep up there all white—snap them. They are majestic animals."

Beth excitedly reached for her camera and started shooting. It amazed her how the bighorn sheep climbed the rocky mountain and stood on almost nothing. She supposed they never fell, but didn't see how they could help it. Right up the steep mountain the sheep climbed once they spotted the strangers getting too close. This sure made the ride home very interesting. What stately animals those white sheep were.

A little ways further, Josh pulled across the street into a pull-out and they all stepped out and looked at the Cook Inlet view. Spectacular! There wasn't any other word that fit the scenic view.

As they drove through Anchorage, the travelers were ready to stop for lunch even though it was a little early. Beth asked,

"Couldn't we come down here and go shopping one of these days? There are so many stores to choose from."

"I think it is a great idea for you and Candice to drive down here and shop. But you might want to plan on staying overnight as it's quite a drive," answered Josh.

"You mean you're not interested?"

"Not to just go shopping. Now if you have another reason to go down to Anchorage other than shopping, I might be interested. There are a lot of good stores in Fairbanks for my shopping needs."

"Beth, don't worry. You and I will plan on coming down one day for shopping and we'll stay all night and have a good time. The men are too old for all that walking so we'll do it by ourselves," Candice laughed as she made the statement.

"That sounds like a great idea to me," Beth admitted.

One more time, Josh pulled the motor home over. "Beth, look over there at that tree."

Beth did and then her eyes widened. The trees were full of bald eagles. It looked like there might be forty or more eagles. In California if someone saw one bald eagle they thought that was something. She put the camera on long range and started clicking.

"If you watch for them you'll see a lot of eagles all over the place," Lonnie assured her. "They look so regal soaring through the skies. They are amazing to watch."

"What is that other bird over on the ground in front of that tree?" Beth asked pointing to a tree close by.

"That is called a puffin. Puffins are also plentiful up here. They like the Alaskan weather," Josh answered. "Say Lonnie, are you about ready to drive this vehicle? I think I need a little rest."

"Sure thing. Everybody ready to go or do we still have some eagle and puffin gazers we need to wait on."

"We're ready," Candice said as the two ladies climbed back into the motor home. "It makes the trip a little more interesting to stop and see sights along the way."

Lonnie had only driven a few miles when he started to slow down and came to a complete stop at the side of the road.

"What's going on, Partner? Why are you stopping?" asked Josh.

"We have a friendly moose up there that doesn't seem to know if she wants to cross the road or not. She's just standing in the middle of the road."

"Why do you think it's a female," Beth asked and then felt dumb. She knew why.

"Well, Cheechako, it's like this. If they don't have antlers, they are female or very young male. Anymore questions?"

"I knew that, I just spoke too soon since you were blaming females for everything," she retorted.

"Well if you remember right, it was a female that caused all the trouble in the Garden of Eden."

Beth refused to answer Lonnie. He was baiting her and she wasn't going to respond to his nonsense. She never won anyway.

Finally, the moose ran off into the tundra and Lonnie drove on. When they finally reached Fairbanks, everyone was tired and decided to sleep in the motor home one more night. Two o'clock was too early to go in and get into a cold bed.

In the morning, Lonnie and Candice retrieved their car and headed for home. Josh plugged the motor home into the electric outlet to keep the fish frozen which were in the motor home freezer.

Beth walked into the house and decided that she was glad to be home. She was going in the bathroom for a very long hot bath. The showers in the motor home had to be quick and use as little water as possible. Now she was going to sit and soak in the tub right after she ate breakfast. Josh explained that they would unload the motor home on Saturday. He brought in the fillets that were on ice and put them in the freezer and left the rest in the motor home until Saturday.

After Josh had gone to work the next day, Beth was surprised at the knock on the door. When she looked out, she recognized Tara from church. An Indian woman accompanied her. "Come in," Beth said.

"I want you to meet my friend, Sue. She lives a little further up the road and she wanted to meet you. We are on our way to fish for pike. Want to come along?"

"It's nice to meet you, Sue. Sure I'd love to go fishing. Are you going right now?"

"Yes, we have plenty of mosquito spray, just bring your boots and jacket and let's go," Tara said.

The three got into Tara's pickup and drove to the Tanana Flats. Tara even had a fishing pole for Beth. All three ladies soon had their lines in the water. It wasn't long before Beth felt her pole jerk and she pulled in a pike. It was a different looking fish. She picked it up about the time that Tara yelled. "Don't pick it up that way."

It was too late. The pike had bit her. She dropped the fish in a hurry and looked at it. "Fish don't bite."

"Most don't you're right, but pike do bite. Here, I have a bandage for you. I should have warned you, but I just assumed you knew. Congratulations on catching the first one." Tara showed her how to handle the fish to ensure she wouldn't get hurt again. The three ladies were soon ready to leave for home.

"I'm so glad I met you, Sue. I hope to see you again and maybe go fishing with you. I enjoyed the day," Beth told her new friend.

"I'll see you at church," Sue said.

Tara and Sue left promising that they would come again for another fishing trip. Beth liked Sue. She was an easygoing woman who knew a lot about Alaska.

When Josh came home that evening, he looked at the pike sitting in the kitchen sink and then he looked at the bandage on Beth's thumb. He smiled and opened his mouth but before he could say anything Beth spoke.

"Not one word out of you do I want to hear! I went fishing with Sue and Tara and had a good time. The least you could have done was to tell me that there are fish that bite." The wife glared at her husband.

Josh broke down and laughed. "You learn everything the hard way, my sweet Cheechako."

Chapter 23

Stranded on the Island

It was Saturday and both Josh and Beth planned to have a lazy day after they unloaded the motor home and placed the fish in the freezer and the jars of salmon, halibut and clams on the shelves that Josh had provided. Oh, the salmon, halibut and clams, whether they were canned or fillets, were going to be good eating and she wasn't going to wait until winter to cook some. Beth was going to spend some time reading the two cookbooks to find the right recipes for salmon and halibut.

Tomorrow was Sunday and they would be going out to a restaurant to eat dinner after church. It seemed that that was the usual thing everyone wanted to do. It was fun. The group was growing and now included several other couples that always met with them at the same restaurant. Beth liked going to church. Ever since she had given her heart to the Lord, she was anxious to attend the services. She wondered why her parents never thought it was important. It certainly was to her.

Josh interrupted her thoughts. "Beth, how would you like to fly over to an island and do some fishing? We'll spend the weekend and come back Sunday evening. Does that sound like something you'd be interesting in doing?"

"That sounds exciting. But which island and where would we stay?"

"I have friends on the island I have in mind. Sam and Cheryl live there and I always have a good time with them. Why don't I call and we'll plan on going one week from now?"

"Perfect."

Josh picked up the phone and called his friends on the island and they happily invited him to come. They were a little shocked that he was bringing along a wife, though. They would meet Josh and Beth at the airport on July 30.

Beth had so much fun on the Kenai Peninsula that she figured this would be similar. Although she had all the salmon they possibly could eat, she wouldn't mind having some more to take down to her mom and dad when they went "outside" this winter.

Josh had planted a small garden. It consisted of mostly potatoes, but he had a few other vegetables as well. Beth put on her bug spray and helped him weed the garden. She needed to do something to get some energy. It seemed that she had to push herself to do anything. She was just plain getting lazy.

A few days before it was time to fly over to the island, the phone rang. It was her parents calling. Her mom was so excited that she could barely understand what she was saying.

"Did you say you are coming up here to Fairbanks, Mom?"

"That's right. We plan on being there on the second of August. I hope that will work out for you."

"Yes, that will be good. We're flying over to an island to see some of Josh's friends from the thirtieth to the first of August, so we'll be home. I'll start preparing for your visit. This is exciting. You'll love Alaska, Mom. It's so beautiful. I never get tired of the scenery. I'm anxious to show you around. How long can you stay?"

"We can only stay a week, but your Dad's boss said if he would work on the project on the weekends and accomplish what needed to be done by the deadline, he would pay for us to fly anywhere we wanted to go. We chose Fairbanks. Beth, I'm so anxious to see you. I know you plan on coming down in the fall or winter sometime, but I really miss you and am so anxious to come to Alaska."

"We'll look forward to you coming. It's not even two weeks away." The mother and daughter talked for a while and finally hung up. Beth was so excited. Her mom and dad were coming to Fairbanks and Beth had so many places where she wanted to take her parents and show them the area. When Josh came home, she told him her good news. Josh smiled at her. Beth never appeared to be homesick, but she was pleased that her parents were coming to visit her. He was happy to see his wife so excited.

The night before flying to the island, Beth began packing up what she would need for three days. It shouldn't be too much. Josh said to be sure to take plenty of bug guard. She didn't argue with him. Finally, she was packed. Josh took some of the halibut with them for a gift.

This was the first time that Beth had flown in a small plane. There was only enough room for four people. It certainly was different than the big plane in which she flew to Fairbanks. It seemed to jerk around with every wind that came. Beth kept glancing out the window. They weren't flying as high as the big planes did and she could see a lot more below. In a little over an hour they were at the island and there Cheryl and Sam were waiting for them.

After they greeted one another, they headed for their friend's house. It is a pretty island, thought Beth, with lots of flowers and of course, lots of trees. Cheryl broke into her thoughts.

"What do you want to do, Beth? You want to fish with the men or stay home?" Cheryl asked.

"I love to fish, but if you'd rather not ..."

"Oh, I love to fish, too. I just wasn't sure if you wanted to. We'll plan on going fishing with the men. I think they are planning on going right away."

"That suits me," Beth said. "What do you do for a living so far away from everyone?"

"Sam works for the government and we do have a lot of people on this island. We're not here by ourselves," she said and smiled. Cheryl had been asked that before.

"Oh, so there are a lot of other people on the island. You'll have to excuse me as I'm new to a lot of this. I had never even fished before I married Josh and came to Alaska. I just love the fishing but I like the catching more," Beth laughed.

"I hear you. You'll do a lot of catching here. We're not as fished out as they are in some of the places."

After a cup of coffee and sweet roll, the four moved toward the pickup and headed for the beach. Sam had a twenty-foot boat and they climbed in and rowed out a ways and let the boat drift and they put their lines in the water. In no time at all, Josh had a salmon, then Cheryl had one on. Beth caught the third one and Sam caught the fourth. They fished until they all had three fish each and then rowed back to shore.

Cheryl cooked one of the salmon for dinner. She put in some baked potatoes and made a salad. Again, Beth was sure that everything in Alaska tasted better than in the lower forty-eight.

Beth slept well that night, but she woke up with the same

lethargy that she had felt the day before. This was nonsense, she told herself. The coffee didn't set well so she asked if she could make some tea and Cheryl told her to help herself.

Soon they were on their way to tour the island. Lots of Eskimos lived on the island and they were very friendly. Beth enjoyed talking with some of them as she went through the stores and shops in town. It was a nice little town, she thought. They did a little more salmon fishing and this time from the shore. "What on earth are we going to do with all that salmon?" thought Beth.

It was evening. They planned on going to church with Cheryl and Sam the next morning and fish a little before they headed back home. The pilot was to be here by five and fly them back. Beth was anxious because her parents would be there on Monday morning. She loved the island, but really wanted to see her parents.

When they woke up the next morning, Beth heard a lot of noise going on outside. It sounded like the wind. She jumped out of bed and looked out the window. There was a storm and a half brewing and the wind was about to blow over some trees. It appeared that it already had knocked some down. It was raining so hard, how would they ever find their way to church?

Beth walked into the kitchen where all the others were gathered around. No one was dressed for church. She was puzzled at the grave look on Josh and Sam's face. "What's going on?" she asked.

"Beth, we won't be going to church this morning. It's too dangerous to get out in wind like this. And the rain makes it all the worse to see where we are going. We'll have to just stay in and play some games or watch some television. Not much else we can do," explained Cheryl.

"It won't hurt us to have a slow day after all the fish we

caught yesterday. We can just visit until our pilot comes back to take us home," Beth suggested.

"Hon, we won't be going back tonight," Josh said slowly. "The storm is going to last through tomorrow and maybe even two days after that. You can't fly small planes in wind like this. The wind is so strong the planes would just crash. We have to wait till the weather clears up and the wind dies down."

Beth eyes watered. "But we have to go. My parents are going to be there tomorrow. We have to fly back today or in the morning at least. Who is going to pick up my folks at the airport?"

"I've called Lonnie. He and Candice will pick up your folks and entertain them until the weather clears and we can fly back. I'm sorry you will miss a couple of days of their visit, but that's life in Alaska."

"That's the first part of Alaska life I haven't appreciated," she said in a shaking tone doing everything she could to keep the tears back.

Cheryl poured her a cup of coffee, but it turned her stomach. "I'm sorry, Cheryl, but I need some tea. Josh can drink this cup of coffee."

Josh took the coffee and gave her his cup and she made the tea. He looked at his wife, but said nothing.

"Are you not feeling well?" Cheryl asked.

"Oh, I've been a little lethargic and coffee seems to disagree. I think it's just some bug I'll get over sooner or later. I sure don't want to pass it on to anyone. I'm not really sick, though. Just feel out of sorts and that news Josh gave me didn't help either. I've so looked forward to mom and dad coming. But, as long as we get home for at least a day or two visit I'll be all right."

The next morning the storm was just as bad as it had been

the day before. Sam didn't even try to make it to his job. The police had made an announcement on the local television that no one should go out in the storm unless it was an emergency. Sam took them at their word. His job certainly could wait another day or two.

"Can I call Mom and talk with her?" Beth asked.

"Sure. That's a good idea."

Beth punched in the numbers of their phone and her mother answered. "Hello, Beth, nice to hear from you. Sorry that the weather is keeping you over there, but don't worry about us. Candice and Lonnie have a plan for today and tomorrow to keep us busy. They are taking us somewhere called Alaska Land and we're going to eat there. There were several other places they suggested for the next day. So just don't worry about us and come back when the weather is better."

Beth talked for a while and hung up. How come she was the only one upset by all this? Her parents sounded like they were having the time of their lives without her. She hurried to the bathroom to hold the tears in check. She had to stop this. She was a grown woman and could face disappointments. What on earth was the matter with her? She would see her folks in another day or two and she should be glad that her parents were happy and having a good time with Lonnie and Candice.

Tuesday's weather was a little better. The pilot called and said he thought by Thursday morning he could fly them back. Thursday? That left only left three days to be with her parents, but it was better than nothing.

Chapter 24

A Visit with Mom and Dad

As it turned out, it wasn't safe to fly until Friday. Early Friday morning the pilot flew Beth and Josh back to Fairbanks. Lonnie was at the airport to pick up the once-stranded couple. Beth's mom and dad escorted him.

Beth gave her parents each a hug and told them how sorry she was that she couldn't have been home sooner. They all stepped in the car and headed for home.

"Oh, Darling, don't worry about it. We've had so much fun with your friends and have seen things we never saw before. We've been all over Fairbanks. We even took a trip down the river and saw dog mushers and Eskimo villages. It was great. You don't need to worry about us. We've had a great time."

"Okay, Mom. I was hoping to be with you when you took the trip down the river, but I'm glad you got to do that even if I missed it."

"Candice and I and you are going shopping today, Beth. Is that okay?"

"Sure, are you looking for anything special?"

"Oh, I want to take back some of the Alaskan things like the Alaskan plates, cups, just a few souvenirs. We've been so busy seeing Alaska that we haven't done any shopping," Jean said.

"At least I'll get to go shopping with you. I take it you've already had your breakfast. When did you want to go?"

"Candice is going to pick us up in an hour. So that will give us time to have a cup of coffee and relax a little."

The coffee was all made and Jean poured her daughter a cup. Beth took one smell and knew it wasn't going to work. She got up and made herself a cup of tea. She put some toast in the toaster. That sounds good, she thought. No butter, just toast. Whatever this bug was she had, she sure would like to get rid of it. Although, she was thankful that she didn't feel sick.

Jean raved on about how beautiful the house was. The men were outside talking and making plans of their own for the day. Beth pointed out all the features and then asked her mom how Josh could have received her college graduation picture. Her mother laughed. "Sarah saw it one day and asked for a copy to send to Josh. I gave it to her and had another one made for me." Jean paused and then asked, "Beth, why does Josh have such a big house?"

"He told me it was because he wanted a place big enough to hold a dozen kids. I told him that it seemed that he was planning on adopting a lot of kids. We do want to have children but I wanted to get used to all the country first. We went dip netting and only Alaskan residence can do that. So next year, I'll be an Alaskan resident and I can dip net. It looked like so much fun."

"I'm so glad you are happy here, Beth. You look a little pale, though. Are you feeling all right? I've never seen you pass up a cup of coffee before."

"I'm all right. I think I just have a bug or something. I'm not really sick, just tired and coffee doesn't set well. I guess I have a little stomach problem. Something I ate, probably."

Candice was at the door and the three were on their way to the different stores to spend the day shopping. Candice announced that they wouldn't be home until late and told the two men they were on their own for lunch. "We're going to have lunch in town," she said and drove the car down the road.

"Look, Jean, there's another moose right over there." Candice stopped the car and everyone stepped out. Jean was staring at the moose.

"They are so big. I never imagined them being this big. I think huge is a better word for them. Sure wouldn't want to pick a fight with one."

Candice said very slowly, "I think we better get back in the car right now."

Beth looked up and there was a black bear down the road. "Mom, get into the car. There's a bear down the road coming toward the car. It's a mama bear and there's her baby very close to us. We need to get out of here. We're separating the mama bear from her cub and that's a dangerous thing to do."

They drove past the bear that was running toward its cub, then stopped the car and looked back to see how things were going. "Black bears usually don't attack humans unless they are very hungry or you mess with their cubs and the female bears get very upset if you even get near their cubs," Candice explained.

Finally, they headed for town and reached the shops in Fairbanks. Candice told Jean she was the one to tell them in which stores she wanted to shop. They shopped till noon and then had some lunch. Beth didn't feel that she was over the bug as yet, so she ordered a plain sandwich and a cup of tea.

"Is that all you are eating, Beth? That's not enough to keep a bird alive," her mother remarked.

"I'm having a hard time shaking this bug. Another day or two and I'll be all right. This is all that even sounds good to me."

About three o'clock they decided they had had enough shopping. Jean had bought about every souvenir she really liked. She announced that she would ask her husband to make some shelves just for Alaskan souvenirs.

Sunday, her parents went to church with Beth and Josh. They shook hands with everyone and were surprised at the friendly greetings. On the way home, her parents didn't even mention the service. Beth had put a roast in the oven with the potatoes and carrots and onions so they didn't go out for lunch with their group of friends.

At the table, she wanted so much to start the conversation about the church service. It was so good and the minister's sermon was inspiring. What did her parents think about the service?

Finally, her dad brought up the subject. "That minister preached on the very subject that Lonnie was talking about with us the other day. I was amazed. The minister made getting to heaven sound just a little too simple. I was raised a little different than that. If you wanted to go to heaven, you had to work your way there. That's what I was taught."

"Did the minister change your mind about that, Dad?" asked Josh.

"Well, he read it all out of the Bible. It sounds so simple. Do you two go to church much or was it just for us?"

"We go every Sunday, Dad, and we loved it. We believe what the minister said. You don't earn your salvation. It is free. You have to repent and believe that Jesus died on the cross for your sins and accept Him as your Savior. It's that simple," said the daughter hoping a light would open up for her parents.

"I need to do a little more thinking about it. The Sweenys go to church every Sunday and they have often asked us to go, but it just never seemed that important. We lived good lives and never cheated anyone. If your good outweighs your bad, you get to go to heaven. That's what I've been told."

"Did you find a scripture to back that up?" asked Josh.

"That's the problem. Everything the minister said just threw all my beliefs right out the window. He was quoting scripture that sure didn't agree with my beliefs. I always believed the Bible even though I never read it. Now, that's a ridiculous statement, isn't it?"

"Think about it, Dad, and get that Bible out and read it—start in the New Testament. I have a booklet that you could look at. Let me get it for you." Josh stepped into his library and brought out a small booklet and handed it to Matthew. "You might find this interesting."

Jean spoke up. "Candice and I had a good talk. I believe that minister was right. I used to go to church years ago when I was a child and I remember hearing things like this. I'm going to start going with Sarah. We've talked a few times, but I never got around to going with her to church."

Beth was excited. She wanted her parents to know the Lord and it seemed they were open to it. If not now, perhaps when they went back home, they would go to church with the Sweeneys.

Tomorrow her parents had to leave. Beth only had part of Friday, Saturday, Sunday and Monday morning to spend with her parents. She was disappointed but at the same time thrilled to think that Lonnie and Candice were such good witnesses to them.

Beth didn't sleep too well that night. She got up to get something for her stomach. Whatever they had for supper didn't set well. Finally, she made a run to the bathroom and barely made it before all her dinner came up. Afterwards Beth put the pot on for a cup of tea. It was midnight and she noticed that her parents' light was still on. They were always in bed by ten o'clock and she was curious what they were talking about.

Finally, her stomach settled down and she headed back to bed. Josh was sleeping and she didn't wake him so she slipped into the bed as quietly as she could. The next morning, she was the last one up. Josh had to go to work and he was gone by the time she got up. Her parents were waiting for her to arise and visit with them. Mom had made the coffee and poured her a cup.

"I don't think I can face that coffee this morning, Mom. What would you like for breakfast?"

"Josh fed us. We had some of his blueberry waffles and they were good. There's the batter to make you one," Jean suggested.

"I just want some toast. I sure slept in. I wish Josh had awakened me."

"He said you never slept in and so he thought you must need the sleep. Beth, Josh prayed with both of us before he left. We both accepted Christ as our Savior. We read that booklet he gave us and it made sense to us. We are both so pleased to know the truth. We were disappointed that we didn't get to spend much time with you, but somehow it all worked out." Jean walked over and gave her daughter a hug. "I'm so glad we came to Alaska."

Beth took her parents to the airport and watched them walk toward the aisle where they had to go to board the airplane. She could go no further so she hugged them both goodbye and told her parents that she would see them in a few months. Josh wasn't quite sure if it would be October or January.

The daughter felt very lonesome when her parents left. They

did get to see the things that she wanted them to see, but she wasn't the one that took them around to see the sights. A few tears filled her eyes as she drove home. She felt a little cheated and yet she felt glad that they had found the Lord. Beth had always considered herself a reasonable person but lately, she was moody. "It's got to be this bug I've got that makes me grouchy and upset," she said to herself.

When Josh came in from work, she went over and hugged and kissed him as was her usual greeting. "What's for dinner?" he asked.

"What sounds good to you?" she asked.

"How about some fried salmon and biscuits with lots of butter and maybe a potato salad with plenty of mayonnaise?"

Beth thought about the greasy food, her stomach turned and she ran for the bathroom and heaved. Josh hurried in there beside her.

"This is the second time I've heaved. I was up at midnight loosing my supper. I wish I could get over this bug I got and whatever it is makes me so moody. I've never been a moody person before. I cried because I missed those days of Mom and Dad's visit. That's so silly. I usually take things like that in my stride. What ever this bug is, I just want to get rid of it!"

"You will," said her husband.

"Yeah, but when? It started when we were on the island, no a little before that. I couldn't even stand the smell of coffee. I want no butter on my toast. How long do you think it will be before I get rid of this bug?"

"I'd say in about seven more months. Then the little bug will come crawling out and we can name him Josh Jr. or Elizabeth, Jr." Josh was doing everything he could to keep from smiling.

"You think I'm pregnant?"

"I know you're pregnant."

"How?"

"Count, Beth. When was the last time you had a visit from Mother Nature?"

"Oh, it has been at least two months or more. I've been so busy that I forgot to take notice. Do you really think I'm pregnant?"

"Yep, I do. And I think you should make a doctor's appointment and have it confirmed and follow the doctor's advice. Doctors usually give pregnant women some vitamins to take. Ask Candice about doctors. She has a lady doctor she raves about. You might prefer that."

"I will. Okay, I'll call her tomorrow. In the meantime, I don't think I can fry you any salmon for supper."

"I really didn't want any. I just wanted to make you realize you were pregnant. I've known for almost a month but didn't want to say anything in case I was wrong."

"You, wrong? Never!" she said sarcastically. Beth looked at her husband wondering what he was thinking. "Josh, how do you feel about having a baby so early in our marriage?"

"I think it's wonderful. After this one you'll only have eleven more to go."

Beth picked up the sofa pillow and threw it at him. She said nothing else but sat and glared at him.

After he quit laughing, he asked, "Beth, how do you feel about having a baby now? Honestly, how do you feel?

"Truthfully, I hope you're right and I am pregnant. I rather like the idea. Won't our parents be thrilled? I think a grandchild is the reason they wanted us to get married in the first place," she laughed. "But don't say anything until we are sure about it, okay? I don't want them to get their hopes up and have to tell them I'm not pregnant. Just wait until we know for sure."

"Beth, your mother told me you were pregnant. I was pretty sure you were but I didn't agree or disagree with her."

"Just what did she say? She didn't say anything to me except that I looked pale."

"She said, 'Son, I think your wife looks pregnant. I've never seen her pass up coffee. She likes lots of butter on her toast. These are all signs of a pregnant woman. Is she pregnant?' I told her if you were you had said nothing to me. She looked at me and then dropped the subject. I think she knew I was dodging the question. I was surprised she didn't say something to you."

"Well if my mom guessed you can count on your mom knowing already. There is no such thing as keeping secrets around here. Next Candice will ask me if I'm pregnant and if so why didn't I tell her."

"No, she already asked me," laughed Josh. "She said you looked pale and were fussy what you ate and wondered if you were pregnant. I told her you hadn't mentioned it to me yet."

Beth shook her head and said nothing more. There was no such a thing as a secret in Alaska.

Chapter 25

The Beautiful Fireweed

"Josh, what are those beautiful pinkish flowers that seemed to be everywhere you look? They sure brighten up the scenery."

"Those are fireweed plants. The Eskimos claim that when the flowers reach the top of their stem, then cold weather is on its way. If you notice, they are not flowered all the way up. And by the way, I have some fireweed jelly you might like to taste. It's delicious. Want to pick some of the flowers and try making the jelly?"

"Yes, let's do."

They found a grocery plastic bag in the car and picked enough flowers off the fireweed to satisfy Josh. "I do believe that will be enough for a batch. Now we have to go home and make it."

"It's so nice out that I almost hate to go back to the house. It's such a beautiful day."

"Summer is usually pretty nice unless it turns out to be a rainy summer and then people do get a little upset. But normally, we have nice summers. It makes up for the long winters. And there is so much to do in the summer time that it goes by a little too quickly, at least for me."

Driving home, Beth watched for the moose. You saw them

almost every day. You just had to be on the watch for them, or you would hit one with the car. Beth now loved to see the moose. She thought she wouldn't even mind if Bruce decided to stick her head in the kitchen window to say hello. It was just that first time when she was not used to the moose and that female moose took her by surprise. She laughed as she thought about it. She had had a few scary times since she came to this country.

Beth watched as Josh made the fireweed jelly. It was beautiful and tasted every bit as good as it looked. Beth loved to look at the canned fish, jam, and jelly. It was something they had accomplished together.

A week later the phone rang and it was Candice on the other end of the line. "Beth, the blueberries are ready to pick. Are you up to it? If you are I'll be right over."

"Let's go for it. I've been waiting for this ever since you told me about them. What do you want me to bring with me?"

"Nothing. I'll take care of everything. I have several buckets to pick in and when they get a little over half full we change buckets so we don't squash the berries. I'll be right there."

True to her word, Candice drove in the driveway five minutes later. The two climbed into the pickup and drove a few miles and then headed up a long hill. Just as they reached the top and turned the corner, there was a huge patch of blueberries. The patch must have taken up at least five acres or more.

Beth loved the smell of Alaska wild blueberries. She even loved the taste. She surveyed the area. There were other berry pickers there but plenty of room for everyone. It was about 70 degrees and was a nice day to be outside. The blueberries were only a few inches off the ground so she could get on her knees and just pick away. It didn't take long before she needed to change buckets. She noticed that Candice was on her third bucket.

"How are you doing, Beth? You're not getting too tired or anything?"

"Now don't baby me, Candice. I haven't been to the doctor yet. You don't know why I even want to go to the doctor. I'm perfectly healthy."

"Oh, I know you are healthy. But I want you two to stay healthy," she said grinning.

"Oh, you are so funny. I probably am pregnant, Candice. I have all the signs. But I won't know for sure until next week when I see your doctor. I'm glad it's a woman doctor. It'll make things easier for me. I've never been sick in my life and only went to doctors to get vaccine shots. Going to Dr. Eileen Beeson will make me more at ease."

When they returned home, Candice showed Beth how to make the blueberry jelly. She sent Beth for jars and they washed and poured boiling water in them. Then she showed her the pectin and what the directions said and let Beth do the rest. Carefully, she washed the berries and put them on to boil. Afterwards she strained them and took the amount of juice required and followed the directions. When it was all done, Beth smiled. The jelly looked so pretty. It tasted even better.

They put most of the berries in freezer bags and into the freezer. Candice showed Beth where the blueberry muffin recipe was. "I'll make blueberry muffins for dinner tonight," she announced to Candice. "Why don't you and Lonnie come over for dinner?"

"What a nice idea. I'll bring some steaks for the barbecue

and you throw in some baked potatoes and make a salad and we'll be all set."

"Oh, Candice, that sounds great."

Candice left and Beth started preparing her potatoes for the oven. By the time Josh came home, Lonnie and Candice were all ready grilling the steaks on the barbecue and the potatoes were done. Beth was just pulling the blueberry muffins out of the oven. Josh looked up and smiled.

"I take it somebody was blueberry picking today. Those smell so good. I hope you froze a lot of them. They taste even better in the winter time."

The steaks tasted good to all of them. Beth quit asking if they were moose steaks or beef. She couldn't tell the difference. She had most of her meal down when she stood up and ran to the bathroom.

"I'll be right back, folks. Just keep eating. My wife has a tender stomach," Josh said with a smile. They both nodded but said nothing.

"Am I ever going to get over this? I hate this upchucking! I should have known better than to eat so much, but everything tasted so good."

"Most people get over this part of it by the time they are four months. The doctor will give you something that will help and tell you what is best to eat so you don't get sick. We'll just trust that in another month you'll be fine."

Josh and Beth walked back in the room. "So, when is the baby due?" Lonnie asked without a blink. Lonnie was blunt.

Beth didn't answer him. She made herself a cup of tea and sat down at the table and covered the steaks with a lid. She couldn't even stand to look at the meat. They talked about other things but before they left, Lonnie whispered to her as he stepped out of the house. "I'd guess another six months or so." He left laughing.

Some day she would get even with him—some day for sure.

Candice came over the next week and took her to the doctor. Now that Candice knew, Beth wanted her to come along. Beth was nervous about going to the doctor, but when she met Dr. Beeson, she relaxed. The doctor explained what she was going to do before she even examined Beth. The doctor made her feel so comfortable about everything.

After the examination, Dr. Beeson said, "I believe that you're close to four months pregnant. You are in very good health, Beth, and you should have no problem carrying this baby." The doctor gave her some medicine to help settle her stomach whenever she had something to eat. She also advised her which foods she should avoid until her stomach problems were over.

That evening when Josh came into the house the first thing he said was, "So when's Josh Junior coming?"

"The baby is due in a little over five months according to the doctor. And she said I was in good health and everything was fine. Dr. Beeson is a nice doctor, Josh. She made the whole examination so easy. I'm so glad you recommended her."

Beth called her mom. She knew exactly what her mom would say. Something like, yes, I knew you were pregnant when I was up there.

"Hello Mom, how's everything? How's Dad?" Beth asked.

"Your dad and I are fine. And how are you doing? Are you feeling a little better? You really should go to the doctor, Beth."

"I did, Mom."

"And he told you that you were pregnant?" she asked.

"Something like that," Beth said almost laughing.

"I knew you were pregnant when I was up there. You looked pregnant. And coffee is usually the first thing pregnant women give up when they are having trouble with their stomach. We are going to be grandparents and we couldn't be happier. We want to get some of the things you need for the baby, Beth. So don't be surprised if you get some packages now and then."

Beth's mom had explained that she would confirm it with the Sweenys. Evidently, she had already told her the news. "Everyone knew I was pregnant before I did," Beth thought.

Chapter 26

The Moose Disturbance

As soon as the low bush and high bush cranberries were ready to pick, Beth was ready to go. She had planned to go with Candice, but it was Saturday and Josh suggested that he would take her. Beth was putting on a little weight and knew it wasn't going to be easy to pick berries kneeling down and getting up, but she so enjoyed blueberry picking that she didn't want to miss picking the low and high bush berries. It seemed to her that these were funny or strange names for berries.

This should be all the more fun because Josh was going. He had a way of making everything they did together enjoyable. As she was thinking about it, she thought how glad she was that she had married Josh. He was the best! At times when she was home and dated some of the men, she never could find any that she would care to marry. She wondered if she was just too picky. Then Josh came along and she was glad she was picky. He was exactly what she wanted.

Josh picked up about four gallon buckets and put them in the pickup. "Better take a hat, Hon, as the sun is pretty warm. Sometimes it gets as hot as 90 degrees in the summer in Fairbanks. And after the winter, that can feel pretty warm. Right now it's just under 70 degrees. Enjoy it as you can, as cold weather is just around the corner."

Beth went back in the house and found her cap. It was just a baseball cap, but it was her favorite. On it read, "You can agree with me or you can be wrong." She got a lot of comments on that.

Josh drove quite a ways from home to find his favorite low and high bush berries. He had picked berries for years and knew the best place to go. When he finally stopped, Beth looked around and saw several bushes with small reddish orange colored berries. She wondered if that was the high bush berries because they were up higher off the ground than the blueberries were. When she asked Josh, he said she was right. Then he showed her the low bush cranberries that were right down on the ground.

As she thought how in the world she was going to get down there and pick berries, Josh had a suggestion to make. He suggested that he would pick the low bush cranberries and she could pick the high bush since they grew on big bushes. Well, she sure wouldn't argue about that. She was very relieved. Picking blueberries low on the ground back a month ago was fine, but it would be harder to do now.

Josh pointed to the high cranberry bush she had seen and suggested that was a good place for her to pick. Beth took her bucket, walked over to the bush and started picking. Oh, these didn't smell very good. Smelled a little like dirty socks.

"Are you sure these high bush berries are okay to eat. They smell awful. I don't think I'd care to eat any jelly made from them," she stated emphatically.

"You had some on your pancakes this morning."

"That delicious jelly came from these old smelly berries? Okay, I'll pick away." She glanced at Josh and he was down on his knees all but crawling on the ground picking the low bush cranberries.

"They really are low bush berries, aren't they Josh? You're right down on the ground. At least the blueberries were a little ways off the ground. I'm glad you suggested that I do the high bush berry picking. It's much easier on my big stomach that seems to grow by leaps and bounds every day."

"Oh, you're skinny yet. Just you wait until another three months. Then you'll know what fat is," laughed Josh.

"Maybe I'll watch my diet and not get too fat!"

"Keep on dreaming," he said.

They picked berries in silence for a while. After a bit Josh asked, "How are you doing? Do you have your bucket about full?"

"Yes, but I have more to pick."

"I've got about all we need of the low bush cranberries. If you have your bucket full, that should be enough."

"There are so many berries left on this bush and I want to pick them all. I want to get another bucket and pick a little more."

"We can only use so many, Miss Berry Picker. Don't be self-ish. If you have that bucket about full, that will be plenty."

"Just a few more minutes, please," Beth begged.

Josh was glad Beth enjoyed picking the berries. There really was no hurry, so he brought her another bucket and took the full one to the pickup. While he was at the pickup he thought he heard something. All of a sudden he heard a terrible scream coming from his left side. He looked up and saw a huge male moose some distant away but coming on the run. Then he heard a scream coming from the right side and saw another male moose heading right toward the first moose he saw. A female moose was just off to one side of them. Then he realized that Beth was right in the middle of where the two would meet.

Trying hard not to yell too loud to draw attention to himself or his wife, Josh exclaimed in a frightened voice, "Beth, right now back out of there and head toward me. Don't run but just gradually back out of the way of those two moose."

When she heard the terror in Josh's voice, Beth turned pale and slowly backed away as her husband told her to. It didn't seem that she could move, she was so frightened, but somehow she was backing up. When she heard the screams of the moose, she hadn't paid a lot of attention to them. Beth just figured it was some wild animals and went on picking until she heard her husband's frightened voice.

Beth looked up and saw the moose heading right toward her. She kept backing up faster now and heading for the pickup. When she got to their vehicle, she dropped to the ground and let the tears fall. She could never remember being so frightened in her life. "Thank you, God," she prayed.

Josh came over and helped her stand up on very shaky legs and put her in the pickup. Once she was sitting inside, he gave her a hug. "Let's get out of here, Beth," he exclaimed. "We don't want those moose thinking this pickup is another contender for the female moose." As they watched they heard a crash. The two moose had hit head on and were locking antlers while the female moose leisurely picked at the grass. There went the rest of her high bush berry patch. The moose were totally destroying it. But at least she wasn't in the middle of it. She shuddered just thinking about what could have happened if Josh hadn't called to her.

"One day this week we'll come back here. By then the moose will be gone. I'm just interested in what this place will look like when those two moose get through fighting over the female. When they are in a fighting mood, it's too dangerous to stay and watch them. Beth, I was scared to death. By the time I got to you, that moose would have been there and it would have been too late for either of us. I'm glad you had sense enough to back out and get out of the way. If you had run, the moose might have come after you. As it was, he didn't pay any attention to you. He just wanted to get to that other bull moose." Josh paused and then added, "I think I gained some gray hair over this."

"I think when we come back I may just stay in the pickup. I'm not too sure I want to take a chance running into those two moose again."

"Usually you know the moose are around because you hear them chomping through the woods making noise. I was too busy picking berries to notice them and by the time I did, I hollered. It scared the liver out of me," he said.

As they drove home, Josh told her about another time when two bull moose were fighting and got their antlers locked together and couldn't free themselves. The people who found the moose called the animal control office. Two officers came out and sedated the animals and then proceeded to saw off the antlers until the moose could free themselves once they were awake.

As Beth listened to the fascinating story, she gradually calmed down from her experience with the moose. "I'm rather glad I wasn't there to see that," she informed her husband.

The berry picker looked at all the berries. She was pleased. When they returned home they were going to make high bush cranberry jelly and low bush cranberry jam.

"We will also freeze some of the low bush cranberries for muffins and waffles this winter," Josh said.

"Won't you freeze any of the high bush cranberries?"

"No, they wouldn't taste good. Besides they have a huge seed in the middle of each one. They will smell terrible while they are cooking until you drain the juice off of the berries and then the juice smells much better," Josh exclaimed.

Beth really enjoyed making the jam and jelly with her husband. He knew what he was doing. Being a bachelor all those years, he had to learn to cook. That sure made him a better husband.

The next morning, Josh had a new proposal. "It's hunting season and I'm taking two days off so we can get us a moose for winter. Want to go hunting with me?"

"Why are you going hunting when you have a moose right in the back yard you could shoot?"

"You don't expect me to shoot my pet moose, do you?"

"Why not?"

"She's part of the family. Besides, Bruce is a female. I'm looking for a male. That's what the tag says I have to get. Want to go with me?"

"What do we do?"

"We take the pickup up where I know there are several moose. Lonnie and Candice are going too. We only need one moose between the four of us. We usually get it the first day we go. Sometimes Lonnie and I walk around quietly. We have two-way radios so we can call each other if a moose is in the area. You ladies can stay in the pickup or get out as you wish."

"If Candice is going, so am I. I suppose I should dress for the cold although it isn't too cold out yet."

"Take extra clothes in case."

The next day the four headed for the hills to hunt for a bull moose. All the time Beth had been up in Fairbanks, she had only seen female moose with the exception of the two moose fighting over the female. The males must keep well hidden.

When they reached their destination, the two men started out in different directions. Candice and Beth sat in the pickup for a while and then stepped out and stretched. They looked around at the scenery. Shortly, Beth looked up and saw a big bull moose just off in the trees. "Look Candice, there's a bull moose."

To Beth's surprise, Candice took a rifle out the vehicle along with the shells, loaded the weapon, took careful aim, and pulled the trigger. Down fell the moose. While it knocked Candice backwards some, it did more damage to the moose. Candice casually picked up her two-way radio and called her husband. "You two can stop playing now. Dead-eye Candice has done it again."

All Beth could do was to stare at the calm Candice. Evidently she had been hunting before. Candice had a hunting license that she took out and began writing the date and other pertinent information in the appropriate blanks. Then she headed over to the moose. Beth followed, hesitantly. The moose was dead to the world. Candice had hit him right in the heart. That was one huge moose. She thought Bruce was big, but this moose was bigger yet.

It was only minutes when the men came looking sheepishly and congratulated her. They took out their knives and began to cut open the moose and get rid of the guts. They cut off all four legs and the head and proceeded to put them in the pickup. They now managed to lift the rest of the moose into the vehicle.

The hunters headed for Lonnie's house where they hung up the legs from the tree so the blood would drain and hung up the rest of the moose. Lonnie had every intention of saving the huge antlers. He may not have shot the moose, but he was gong to display those antlers in his garage.

Before Josh and Beth started home, Josh said to Candice, "I'm not taking you next year. We were having the time of our lives out in the woods walking around and visiting and here you come up and shoot the moose and spoil the whole thing." Josh left the house laughing. Candice knew he was kidding.

In two days they would get together and cut up the moose, package it, and divide it between the two couples.

Chapter 27

Visiting North Pole

After going to church and out to eat with their friends, Josh drove home. "I really want to go back and see what those moose did to the area. Shall we go?"

"Sure, I'll go. I bet the place is a mess."

Josh drove the car into the garage and backed out the pickup. The two headed for the woods where they were a few days before. When they arrived, Beth was shocked.

"It's just like I thought it would be," Josh said.

The ground was plowed up for several yards around where the two moose had fought. Beth and Josh walked through the plowed ground.

"There's no more cranberry bush. What will we do for high bush cranberries next year?" Beth asked.

"There are high bush cranberries all over this country. I liked this place because I could get both types of berries in one place, but not anymore. You wouldn't even know there was ever a high bush cranberry bush there. Would have been something to see the fight, but I didn't want them to charge the pickup and we can't go as fast on this back road as those moose can run."

They came back home for a quiet afternoon. Beth picked

up the newspaper and thumbed through it. "Josh, have you ever read these police reports?"

"Sure I've read them, almost every day. Why?"

"I've read them and I just can't believe them. They catch these drunk drivers and take away their license. They drive anyway and they get caught again. They extend the time before they get their license back, as if that was going to do any good. If they are driving without a license because it was taken away from them, why don't they put them in jail or something? It's as if they weren't paying any attention to the police at all. It's a good thing I'm not the police. One time only and then the drunks would end up in jail," Beth said adamantly.

"Boy, I hope you're never on the jury if I have to go to court," Josh laughed.

"Well, don't you think that's terrible they don't do anything more about the drunk drivers?"

"Yes, I do, but they wouldn't have enough jail space to put them all in. Some of them have a wife and children to take care of. The judge gets real soft with some of them so they can feed their family. Otherwise welfare has to feed them. As long as there is alcohol available, there doesn't seem to be a good solution when it comes to drunk drivers. You just want to make sure you aren't on the road with one."

Beth almost finished reading the paper when it dropped from her hands. She had been lying on the couch and finally dozed off. She felt someone shaking her.

"Beth, Beth, wake up. Dinner is on the table."

"What?"

"Beth, you have slept the rest of the afternoon. It is six o'clock and I have dinner all ready for you. Let me help you up. Let's eat, now that you don't have any trouble keeping your food down."

Beth shook her head and tried to wake up. She had slept hard. She headed for the dining room. "It's supposed to be my job to get the meals," she whined.

"I think you are going to need a little help in that department from time to time. You are carrying someone around with you all the time and that can tire you. Sit down and enjoy a meal you didn't have to cook," her husband said and kissed her on the forehead.

Josh was one good cook.

"Beth, you haven't seen Santa Claus House at North Pole, yet, have you?"

"Santa Claus House in North Pole, you are kidding aren't you?" Beth asked frowning. Was this another one of Josh's jokes?

"I've neglected my duties. Next Saturday, we'll go over to North Pole. We should have taken your parents there, but we had such a short time and I forgot. I think that you'll like it. Although you'd think it would be for kids, it's definitely aimed at adults. There are lots of things to buy as well as a Santa Claus whose there year round. You'll love it and I'll bet you that you come home with some things for the baby."

"If there are things there for a baby, I'll bet I do too. We do need to go crib shopping one of these days and get a dresser to put her clothes in," she said grinning.

"His clothes, you meant to say?"

Saturday came and they were off to the Santa Claus House in North Pole. Beth had been surprised that there was a town even called North Pole. It wasn't all that far from Fairbanks and she enjoyed the trip. They pulled into the parking lot and stepped out of the car. It did look like a pretty big place.

Josh opened the door for Beth and she stepped into the building. It did look like a real Santa Claus House. She was impressed. So many things to look at, she was sure that it would take all day to see everything. There were some soft stuffed animal toys that she wanted for the baby. Beth picked up a nice pink fluffy dog.

"You don't want that one," Josh said. "Take the blue one. I don't want Josh, Jr. playing with a pink puppy." Josh looked serious as long as he could and then laughed. "Get the one you want. I'll just have it recovered when the baby gets here."

"Never mind, I'll get the green one, then," Beth said as she stamped her foot. What would Josh do if they had a girl? Oh, he would be fine. It was just a fun thing to pick at each other about whether it would be a boy or a girl. She could see her big old burly husband holding a tiny baby girl. "I'll bet he'd be scared to death," she thought.

Beth noticed the different rooms with different Christmas displays. There were so many Christmas tree decorations. She selected a few and then asked Josh, "Do you put up a Christmas tree every year?"

"I have to because we make the rounds to our friend's houses and everyone examines each tree and we visit. I don't have a choice. I have some decorations, but we could use some more and I'm sure you have your own idea what you would like our tree to look like. Just remember that there will be about six couples coming over to see it."

"That sounds like a good time. Do we go to a different person's house each night, or all in one night?"

"Good question. What we do is go to dinner at the people's houses. We find out who all is going and we figure out the days and have dinner each night at a different person's house. It's always been fun."

"It sounds terrific. I'm going to look for unusual decorations to fix our tree. It should be a great time. I'll be about six months pregnant then—really fat."

The two spent two hours at the Santa Claus House and then headed for a restaurant. "That's quite a tourist attraction they have there," Beth commented.

"It brings a lot of people to North Pole that wouldn't otherwise bother to come. It's not a very big town, but the Santa Claus House attracts about every visitor that has heard something about the shop."

Chapter 28

The Avalanche

Coming into the house with a stack of mail, Josh sat down and opened the letters. He gave the one from Beth's mom to Beth and set the bills aside. There was a letter from Ron Starnes. He'd known Ron for a long time and had some good times with him. He'd never written before as he always called. After reading the letter, Josh put it down and said, "Well, I'll be. I can't believe it."

"Can't believe what?" Beth asked.

"You remember the game warden who we talked to when we were clam digging?"

"Yes, his name was Ron. He seemed like a nice man and was shocked that you were married."

"Well, now Ron is getting married. He's about my age. He wants me to come down for his wedding and be his best man. Are you up to a drive to the Kenai Peninsula?"

"Oh, I'd love to go to the Kenai Peninsula again. It's so nice. I don't suppose the fishing is going on now in October or November."

"No, there won't be any salmon fishing and only the bravehearted take a boat out for halibut fishing this time of year. I like better weather when I go ocean fishing. It will be much cooler than when we were there before. We had a little brush of snow last night but it melted. We will very likely run into some snow. Still want to go?"

"Yes. If for nothing else, I'd like to see the scenery again. Besides, you can't disappoint your friend. It's an honor to be the best man at any wedding. You were sure the best man at ours," she grinned.

"I'll call him and tell him we'll be there. The wedding is on the first of November and we should leave here about three days before. We'll stay overnight somewhere close to Anchorage and then we should be able to make the trip the rest of the way. I don't want you to get too tired."

"Quit babying me. The doctor says I'm doing very well and I'm very healthy. Little Bethany is just fine."

"You mean little Josh. You misspoke that, I'm sure."

Beth kept quite busy the rest of October making baby clothes. Josh had bought her a new sewing machine. She had found some baby patterns and material in town and was having the time of her life sewing. She loved it. Beth was beginning to believe what all their men friends said, "Everything is bigger and better in Alaska." She had sewed many times but never enjoyed it quite so much as she did now.

It was time to leave and Beth was packing what she would need. She was excited about the trip. Josh had reminded her that it was cold and to be sure and take lots of warm clothing. She did just that.

The drive through Fairbanks reminded her of her first trip through the town. The trees were already frosted with snow and the town was white all over. It had snowed quite a bit all through October and the temperature was down to 40 below already. So much for a long fall—it wasn't going to happen. It seemed that they had winter and then spring, fall, and summer all happened in five months time and winter was here again. But it didn't matter. She loved Alaska.

Some of the road was icy and Josh drove very carefully. He had four-wheel-drive as well as studded tires so that would help when the roads were snowy or icy. The two stopped at a small restaurant for lunch and then drove on to Wasilla and selected a motel. Beth was very happy to stop and rest. It was a long drive. It didn't seem this long when they went fishing last summer, but then her stomach wasn't quite so big then either.

Beth loved going through Anchorage. She never did get to do the shopping she and Candice had planned. It seemed that both of them had been too busy to find time to go. One of these days, they would go shopping in Anchorage.

They were not too far out of Anchorage when she heard Josh yell, "Oh, no," and she saw the panic on his face. He stopped the vehicle quickly. Beth was only too glad that she had her seatbelt on. No cars were behind him and Josh tried to back up quickly but didn't quite make it far enough. Josh had seen the avalanche coming and the snow tumbling right down the mountain side and heading directly for their vehicle. Finally, he couldn't back up anymore. He grabbed Beth and hung onto her.

"What just happened, Josh? Where did all this snow come from? We can't even see out of the windows. What's going on?" Beth asked visibly upset over what happened.

Josh held her close and kissed her cheek. "Beth, we got caught in the tail end of an avalanche. I think we'll be just fine, but I need to try to back up just a little. I think I can back out of this snow, if I do it a little at a time and move forward and then back."

Josh honked his car horn and slowly backed up. He went forward and honked again and back up a little further. After the third try he could finally see daylight. He let out a big sigh. He had been quite sure they had been caught only in the last bit of the avalanche but he wasn't positive. Josh was relieved.

It wasn't long before he heard sirens coming his way. A policeman drove up beside their car and rolled down his window. Josh did likewise.

"Sir, are you two okay. I saw you backing out. You both all right or do you need some help?"

"Yes, we are fine. It was a little scary there for a moment, let me tell you. I've seen avalanches before, but never took part in one," Josh said laughing. It might be a laughing matter now but it wasn't earlier. He wasn't sure but that he was still shaking from the experience.

"You might as well go back to Anchorage. You won't be able to get through this mess for sometime," the policeman informed him.

"Sergeant, I'm to be best man at a wedding in Soldotna. They are having the wedding rehearsal tonight. I don't suppose we're going to make it, huh?"

"Probably not in time for the rehearsal, but you might make it a little later this evening. It will take four or five hours to clear the snow from the road. You better pull your vehicle off the road so they can get started. Could you tell me if there were any cars ahead of you close enough to be caught in the avalanche?"

"I don't think so. What do you think, Beth?"

"I'm sure there wasn't. All the cars were going a little faster than we were. I think they were well past the avalanche," she agreed.

"Well, that's good news and we can use a little good news

looking at this mess. I'll tell the workers they needn't worry about anyone being in there. If you are still intending on going to the peninsula tonight, I'd suggest that you drive over to that restaurant a mile back and relax for about four or five hours and then come check it out again. Can you get a hold of your friend?"

"Yes, I'll call him on the cell phone. Thanks officer."

Josh turned the vehicle around and drove back to the restaurant. "Let's take that officer's advice and go into the restaurant and just relax."

As they got out of the vehicle, Beth laughed. The rig was still loaded down with lots of snow. Josh took out a long brush and brushed most of the snow off. "What a trip," he said and laughed. "We might as well laugh as cry, Beth."

When they sat down in the warm restaurant, Josh took out his phone and called Ron. "Say, friend, I may be somewhat late for the rehearsal. Do you suppose you could use a stand-in for me and fill me in when I get there? We got caught in an avalanche—just the tail end of one. I managed to back out of it after a few tries, but they say it will be four or five hours before the road is cleared."

"Don't worry about it. All you have to do is stand by me and make sure I don't faint and hand me a ring. But I'm glad you called and double glad you weren't in the middle of that avalanche. Thank God you weren't!" They talked a little longer and then hung up.

The waitress came by and handed them a menu. "Did you folks see the avalanche down the road?" she asked. "It's visible from here."

"We got a very close look at it," Josh said laughing.

"We got caught in the tail end of the avalanche," Beth explained.

"Really? Oh that sounds dreadful."

"Well, the good Lord took care of us and we got out. I believe He had angels watching out for us," Josh said.

"I'm sure you're right," the waitress commented and left them alone to peruse the menu. After they ate, they looked around the shop next door that had all kinds of Alaskan souvenirs.

"What are those funny looking things," Beth asked Josh.

"Those are called ulu knives. They are handy cutting up meat. That's what the Eskimos use to cut up their moose and other wild game."

"The knives just look odd. Ulu knives, huh—never heard of them before. Guess I learned something more today than what's it's like to be in an avalanche, right?"

"I'd say you learned first hand about avalanches. God was good to us, Beth, and I think you know that. We could have been right in the middle of it. Avalanches kill people every year."

"I know He was watching over us. I'm not sure I should tell my mom about this, she'll want me to come home."

"I'd wait a while. Experiences like this need to be told carefully—especially to parents." After looking around in the souvenir shop for a while, the two headed back to the restaurant. They sat back down at their table and drank another cup of coffee.

Josh looked up and recognized the policeman who was coming in the restaurant. "Hello, how's the removal of the snow coming along, Officer?"

"It's almost done. They made good time. In about a half hour, you can get through. I just wanted to let you know. I wouldn't want you to miss that wedding." The officer said goodbye, filled his coffee cup, paid for it, and left.

"I'll bet that nice warm coffee is going to taste good to him,"

Beth said. "It was nice of him to come by and tell us that we could get through the snow in a half hour. There are a lot of nice people in this big state," Beth said and Josh agreed.

Chapter 29

The Best Man

After the half hour was up, Beth and Josh started back down the road to the Kenai Peninsula. Snow was piled on both sides of the road. It felt as though they were going through a tunnel. There was lots of snow on every mountain they passed. In spite of the fact that Josh was late for the rehearsal, he wasn't speeding down the road. He was taking his time. Beth was glad that he was a careful driver.

They passed Turnagain road and headed through the Chugach Forest. It was always a pretty drive. After a few minutes, they noticed a driver who had passed them going a little too fast was now in the snow bank off the road. Josh stopped the car and asked if he could help them. They readily agreed to the help. Josh retrieved his tow chain and hooked it to the vehicle in the snow bank. In just minutes, the people were out of the snow bank and on their way. They thanked Josh several times.

Finally they reached their destination in Soldotna. They drove to the church where the wedding would be taking place. Josh was glad that there were cars still there. That meant people were still in the church. They hurried into the building to see if they were completely too late. Ron saw Josh and came down the aisle to welcome him and introduced him to Shanda, his bride to be. The rehearsal was over but the groom to be showed him where to stand. All he had to do was walk out with him when the time came, give the groom the ring when told and stand by. It seemed pretty simple to Josh.

The next day, the wedding party headed for the church. Beth watched the bride as she walked down the aisle with her father. The bride must be around 28 or so, Beth guessed. Shanda smiled all the way down the aisle apparently not the least bit nervous. The two made a nice looking couple.

When the ceremony was finished, the wedding party entered the fellowship hall. The bridal group lined up to shake hands with everyone. Shanda was so excited she was bouncing and exclaiming, "I did it. I did it. I really got married."

Beth laughed. She was excited at her wedding, but she didn't know if she was quite that excited. When they stepped outside, it was cold. There was the groom's vehicle covered with Oreo cookies which had been separated and stuck on the car with the frosting and frozen in place. No shoes, or streamers, just Oreos decorated the car plus a sign that said, "Just Married." They did do things different in Alaska, mused Beth.

Josh and Beth stayed overnight with Kirk and Alice before they started on the long journey home. "Beth, how would you like to do a little shopping in Anchorage and we'll spend the night there and be on our way. I've stayed at the Puffin Inn before and that's a good place to stay."

They did a little shopping first and then went to the Red Lobster for lunch and back for a little more shopping. Josh wanted to stop at the book store. Beth was amazed when she stepped into the building. There was even an upstairs. Josh went one way and Beth another. They agreed to meet in two hours. As she looked around, she knew that she could spend the whole day there. Besides books, there were videos and DVDs available. When they left, they both had purchased books and a couple of DVDs.

Josh and Beth left early in the morning to get a head start for the trip home. On the way they met many moose and always gave them the right of way. A few other animals crept across the road. In all, it was an easy trip home. Beth was happy to be back home and away from the avalanche areas.

Coming into the house, Josh heard the answering machine beeping. He pushed the message button. "Hey, Josh, this is Barry. Give me a call."

Josh dialed Barry's number. "Hello, this is Barry Burns."

"Barry, this is Josh. You left me a message."

"I sure did. I intended to call you before. Guess what we did in September?" Barry asked.

"There is no telling what you and your grandson might do," Josh said laughing.

"You were there when my pickup went swimming down the river. Well, would you believe that my grandson had it pulled out of the river, he and his dad worked on it and it is now up and running?"

"No kidding? It still runs. What did it smell like when you pulled it out?"

"You don't want to know. There were some dead salmon in it and a few other dead things. I thought my grandson would never get the smell out, but he did. I had told him if he got it out and fixed it up, it was his. He's so proud of that old pickup. That's a sixteen-year-old for you." Barry was laughing. They talked a while longer and finally said goodbye hoping to see each other next summer.

"Beth, do you know what Barry just told me?"

"No, what did Barry just tell you?"

"That his grandson was able to get the pickup out of the river and after a great deal of work. They now have it in good running condition."

"That's nice," Beth said. "Did they find any salmon in it as the officer said?"

"Yes, and I guess it really smelled."

Looking around her home, Beth decided it was time to do some cleaning and get rid of some of the garbage that had accumulated here and there. She worked most of the morning and was ready for a trip to the dump. "Josh, I'm going to run to the dump and I'll be right back," she said.

"Why don't you take the pickup and drive to the dump?"

"Everybody is a comic," was her reply.

"I can take the garbage to the dump. It's awfully slick out there," Josh suggested.

"Josh, I just want to get out and get some fresh air. I promise to drive carefully and watch out for moose."

Beth threw the sacks in the pickup and drove to the landfill. After she had deposited the garbage, she turned the pickup around. Something happened and before she knew it, the pickup was on its side. She blinked a couple of times and carefully unsnapped her seat belt. Someone must have called the police as she heard the sirens blasting.

The officer stepped out of his car grumbling. These teenage drivers never seem to learn how to drive on ice. He took out his book to write up a ticket for the careless driver. As he walked toward the pickup, he noticed the ice was very slippery. The next thing he knew he was down on the ice with a very sore knee.

Was it broken? He tried to get up and slipped again. Finally he made it over to the pickup and looked inside. His face paled. There sat a very pregnant young lady.

"Are you okay, ma'am?" he asked nervously.

"I'm fine but I don't know if my pickup is and you look like you're hurt. I called my husband and he should be here in a few minutes."

"You are Josh Sweeny's wife, aren't you?"

"Yes, do you know Josh?"

"Everyone around here knows Josh. Well, Mrs. Sweeny, I was going to write you a ticket, but since I couldn't even stand up on this ice, I don't think it would be right to blame you because your pickup couldn't stay upright. I see your husband just drove up."

Josh hurried over to his wife and hugged her. She assured him she was not hurt in the least. "Hi, Sergeant. Can you help me turn this pickup upright? Beth says she is fine and just wants to go home." Josh allowed himself a smile since his wife wasn't hurt.

After rubbing his knee a bit, the sergeant managed to hobble closer to the pickup and help Josh upright the vehicle while they both struggled to keep themselves upright on the slippery pavement. Finally, Josh and Beth were on their way back home. All Josh said to her was that he was so thankful she wasn't hurt and that he thought maybe he should take the garbage to the landfill at least until after the baby came. Beth readily agreed.

November passed and it was getting closer to Christmas. Beth wondered what in the world she could buy her husband for Christmas. He was a man who had everything he wanted all ready. Maybe he could use another nice heavy shirt. He rarely wore a tie. She wanted something special for him but had a hard time thinking what it would be. Beth bought her parents each an Alaskan gift since the two enjoyed Alaska. She bought something for Candice and Vonnie. It was up to Josh to buy something for the men.

"Josh, what do you want for Christmas," Beth asked.

"I want to spend my Christmas with my wife. That's what I want."

"No, I need to buy you something. I can get you clothes, but you seem to have everything you need or want. There must be something. Give me some hints."

"You want me to make this easy for you, huh? Well, what do you want me to buy you for Christmas?"

Beth looked at him. He was just as puzzled about gifts as she was. Now that's funny. "What we could do, is I could get something for me and wrap it up and give it to you and you could get something for you and wrap it up and give it to me. Then after we open them, we could exchange gifts."

Beth glared at him. "That's a crazy idea. There are lots of things you can get for me. Maybe I'll ask Lonnie what he thinks you would like."

"While you are at it, ask Candice what I should get for you."

This conversation was going nowhere. She would find something for Josh. Even if it were a duplicate of something he had.

After Josh left for work the next day, Beth took off for Candice's place. They had planned a shopping spree especially for Christmas. Candice had a good idea what to get for Josh.

"Haven't you noticed his parka? It's worn out. Why don't you find out his size and get him a new one. You could throw in a new shirt or something else."

"Oh, thanks, that's a great idea. I'll do that. It's a wonder he hadn't bought another one already."

Beth had finished her Christmas shopping and was like a kid waiting for Christmas to arrive. The week before Christmas, Josh and Beth spent every night having dinner at a different couple's house. It was great fun. They brought little gift items for each family whose house they visited. It was enjoyable to Beth when the group came to her house. Josh's company always closed down the week of Christmas so he was free. It wasn't too surprising that the gifts the couples brought to her house were all baby gifts.

Christmas morning they had their breakfast first and then opened gifts. Beth opened her gifts from Josh first. There was a brand new beautiful smock with Alaskan decorations on it. She loved it. There was also a very warm bathrobe. Hers wasn't all that warm so she would enjoy that. Then, there was a package of things for the baby, mostly for a boy. Josh loved his new Parka and the shirts she bought. All in all, they had great time opening presents.

The small turkey was in the oven along with the sweet potatoes. She made some light bread buns for dinner. Josh fixed a few dishes. There was much more than the two of them could eat, but they would eat on the leftovers for several days. And they did.

The week went by quickly and New Years Eve was here. Josh and Beth went to the service at their church that would last until midnight. Several people sang solos, read poems, put on little plays. Midnight came quickly. Beth had never before spent such a wonderful time on New Year's Eve. Usually, she was with drinking friends and just tolerated the evening.

January was cold. The thermometer went clear down to 50 below. Beth thought the safest place for her was right in the house.

It still amazed her how everyone plugged their car in whenever they went shopping in the wintertime. She read in the paper where some people's steering wheels got so cold that they burst into pieces. She was definitely glad they had a heated garage.

When February came, Beth was miserable. She was eight months along now and had trouble getting in and out of the easy chair. The doctor assured her all was well. She would be so glad when February was over and the baby was here. Josh said that as soon as she felt it was okay, they would take a trip to visit both of their parents and show off their new little boy. By now they knew it was a boy. She would have to save the little dresses for the next baby. One more time that husband of hers said he told her that it would be a boy she was going to bop him.

The fifth day of March, Beth woke up with labor pains. They felt pretty hard to her although she didn't know that much about it. It was only the middle of the night, but she was worried. She shook her husband and tried to wake him. Finally, he rolled over and asked her if it was time to get up.

"Yes, and I think we better hurry. I'm in labor, Josh, and it is hard labor. We have a ways to drive to get to the hospital." Beth's suitcase had been packed for a month, so all they had to do was dress and go.

This time, Josh drove a little faster than usual. He was in a hurry to get to the hospital in Fairbanks. Each time his wife moaned he'd speed up a little more. He knew he could deliver a baby, as he had to one time, but he sure didn't want to deliver his own. The pains were only three minutes apart. He was relieved when they drove in the hospital emergency entrance. There was a gurney waiting for his pregnant wife. Beth had used the cell phone to call and warn that she was in hard labor and coming to the hospital.

Josh hurried into the delivery room with Dr. Beeson. Ten minutes later he was holding his beautiful son. Beth had looked the baby over and then let Josh hold him. He looked so tiny in Josh's big hands. They were two proud parents.

"What are you going to nickname the baby, Josh. I can't go around saying Josh and neither of you will know who I'm talking to."

"Since he's going to be my buddy, I think I'll nickname him Buddy. Is that all right?"

"Sounds fine to me."

"You need to call Candice and Lonnie. They will want to come and see him. I wonder what they'll have to say."

"They will say that he's the cutest baby they have ever seen. I will call them in a little bit, but I don't think I should wake them up at two o'clock in the morning. How about six o'clock. That should be okay. Lonnie will probably come by before he goes to work. We'll never get rid of Candice."

"She does love babies."

Chapter 30

A Visit Home

Lonnie and Candice were at the hospital as soon as Josh called. Candice was so excited and since the baby was kept in Beth's room, Candice wanted to hold him. She fussed over him and talked baby talk to him. When Josh and Beth brought Buddy home, Candice was right there every day to see him. Beth hadn't realized before how much Candice wanted a baby.

Almost every day Candice brought some item, clothes, or toys for the baby. "He's so cute, Beth. He's beautiful. I hope I'll have one some day. I just have to have patience, I've been told. If you ever need a babysitter, I'm it," she said, meaning it.

"Since I'm nursing him, it will be a while before I can leave him for any length of time, but I'll remember what you promised. The baby sure changed our lives. Before we were just concerned about ourselves and now every waking minute we are concerned about our baby. I love being a mama."

"What do your parents and Josh's parents say about the baby?"

"They are demanding that we bring him home as soon as possible. I want to take him home and show him off. Isn't that terrible? He's sure good. He doesn't keep us up all hours of the night as you've heard people say babies do. Buddy wakes up and nurses and goes right back to sleep. I suppose the next one couldn't possibly be this good."

"When are you going to your folks?" Candice asked.

"When Buddy is one month old, we'll take him down. He should be fine. The doctor said he was in perfect health. That statement made me feel very happy."

"Aunt Candice is going to miss Buddy when you go," Candice said and left for home. Beth sure hoped that one of these days Candice would have a baby.

When little Josh was one month old, they decided it was time to visit the anxious grandparents. It was April and although the weather was cold, it was much warmer now than in January. They bundled the son up and took a good supply of diapers for the young man. Beth was nursing the baby so there would be no problem with bringing food for the youngster.

The trip down to Los Angeles was easy. Little Josh was a good baby and only fussed when he was wet or hungry. Beth never tired looking at her son. She could hardly believe that she was a mother.

When they arrived at the Los Angeles airport, it was no surprise to find all four parents waiting to greet them. Each one was anxious to see their first grandchild. Beth's mother was the first to greet her. She quickly hugged her daughter and then took the baby. Beth was amused. Her mother had always loved babies, but this was different. This was her grandchild, her first grandchild.

Josh and Beth watched as the two grandmothers made over the baby. They declared he was the prettiest baby either one of them had ever seen.

The only time Beth got to hold the baby was when he needed feeding. Her mom or mother-in-law changed the baby and rocked him and even bathed him. They only put him down when he was sound asleep. Sometimes she wondered if they didn't deliberately wake him up just so they could hold him. Sarah spent a lot of time at the Vandermeers home while they were there. Josh took his son over to his dad from time to time.

"Hey, Buddy, how are you doing," Josh said as he was the closest to the baby when he woke up. "How's my big boy?" It appeared to Josh that the boy knew his voice and he smiled. Although there were two grandmothers waiting for him to give them the baby, Josh kept him and sat in the rocker. "It's my turn to hold Buddy," he said and rocked away. The two ladies returned to the kitchen somewhat disappointed.

"I suppose we have to let Daddy hold his son sometime. I just can't get enough of that boy and to think, they have to leave next week. We're going to make a quick trip up there as soon as Matthew gets a vacation," Jean exclaimed.

"Buddy is a sweet baby. It's nice that he doesn't have colic like some babies do. I'll miss him too. I'm hoping we can make a trip up there before too long," admitted the other grandparent.

The two weeks went fast and the three travelers were packed and ready to fly back to Fairbanks.

"Say, Son, are you sure you don't want to leave Buddy here with us. You had that baby so easy. There are four of us who would really enjoy him and you could go back and start on the other eleven children you are going to have." Matthew never even grinned.

"Dream on," was all that Beth said.

"I know we're supposed to obey our parents, but that is going just a little too far," laughed Josh. "I don't think we can live without that boy now. It's a whole different world when you have a baby."

"We know," echoed the grandparents.

The day came when it was time to return to go to Fairbanks. Jean held the baby all the way to the airport. When it was time to board the plane, she had a hard time saying goodbye. The grandmother didn't even try to hide her tears. "We're coming up as soon as your dad gets a vacation," she exclaimed. "If it takes too long before the vacation, I'm coming up alone!"

Matthew looked at his wife and put his arm around her. They had so enjoyed the youngster and now it was going to be an empty house they would return to.

The trip to Fairbanks was an easy one. Lonnie and Candice met them. The first thing Candice did was take the baby. She loved to play with Buddy anytime they came for a visit. Beth watched her with the boy. There was something different about Candice. Candice was pregnant!

When they reached their home and went inside, Beth cornered Candice. "So when is yours due?" she whispered.

"What do you mean?" Candice asked smiling.

"You know what I mean."

"In seven months. I just found out about it when you were gone. I haven't been sick to my stomach or anything. I just went in for my yearly checkup and Dr. Beeson told me I was pregnant. The only clue I had was that I had stopped having visits from Mother Nature, but that wasn't unusual for me. I was stunned but Lonnie was shocked. But after the initial shock, he got over it and he's tickled. I think Buddy made him want to have a baby of his own. We've been married for five years and nothing had happened yet. The doctor told us that all was well and we'd just have to be patient. I tried hard not to be too envious of you when you were pregnant so soon after you were married. But, thank God, we're going to have a baby in seven months."

Lonnie yelled at the two women. "Are you telling tales out of school, Candice?" he asked.

"I didn't have to tell her. She knew."

Beth picked up Buddy and smothered him with kisses. "My little Cheechako," she said to him.

"Oh no, Beth," Lonnie exclaimed. "He's not a Cheechako. He was born in Alaska. You, Mrs. Sweeny, are the only Cheechako in the room."

"I just never win," exclaimed the Cheechako.